THE
ANCHOR
KNOT

securing the knot of truth

The KNOT Series gives a voice to modern social issues that are frequently hushed. The novels untangle struggles and interlock relationships as the characters heal and achieve happiness.

The KNOT Series I

The Trinity Knot
The Zeppelin Bend (sequel to *The Trinity Knot*)
The Hitch (sequel to *The Zeppelin Bend*)

The KNOT Series II

The Shackle (sequel to *The Hitch*)
True Love Knot (sequel to *The Shackle*)
The Anchor Knot (sequel to *True Love Knot*)

THE
ANCHOR
KNOT

securing the knot of truth

DONNALEE
OVERLY

THE ANCHOR KNOT
Copyright © 2023 by DonnaLee Overly

For permission, please contact the author at www.donnaleeoverly.com or e-mail donnaleeoverly@gmail.com.

Printed in the United States of America
First Edition, July 2023

Fernandina Beach, Florida

Cover and Interior design by Roseanna White Designs

The Anchor Knot artwork by DonnaLee Overly

Library of Congress Control Number: 2023907895

ISBN Trade Paperback 13: 978-1-7352517-6-9
E-BOOK: 13: 978-1-7352517-7-6

www.donnaleeoverly.com

This book is dedicated to all women.
May you celebrate your power and know your worth.
&
To my faithful fans for reading The KNOT Series.
With you turning the pages, my journey is sweet.

To My Readers

The King family has been with me for nine years so writing this final novel was bittersweet. I feel as though each character is a member of my family and I am saying goodbye.

As a special gift of appreciation to my readers who have been with me from the beginning of the series, The Anchor Knot contains a few choice references from each of the previous books. My wish is that when you come across these special treats, you'll stop and pause to remember those steps in Gabby's journey.

As readers, we understand and emphasize with Gabby as life throws her some serious challenges, but we also get frustrated with her choices. There's a saying that one learns more from one's mistakes and Gabby puts that to the test. Gabby needs to wiggle out from under her daddy's thumb and find her own way. Hopefully, you saw her grow as the story progressed. With that said, I need to stop and let you dive into The Anchor Knot: securing the knot of truth. Enjoy and thank you again for sharing this journey!

Acknowledgments

This book would not have been possible without the help of many others, and I am extremely grateful. Thank you to girlfriends who provided insight, to the experts who shared their precious knowledge, and to my beta readers. I am thankful for Erin Liles, my understanding editor, and Roseanna White, the designer of this beautiful cover and interior.

A special note of thanks to my family for putting up with me: my husband for his continuous love, reading, and editing; and to my son, Dan, for saving my manuscripts,

just in case I crash my computer. He has awesome IT skills and made me a grandmother!

Readers can contact me through my website www.donnaleeoverly. com. As always, your review on Amazon and GoodReads, or my webpage is always a blessing.

DonnaLee

Love anchors the soul.
An anchor is a reminder of one's roots and origin.

CHAPTER 1

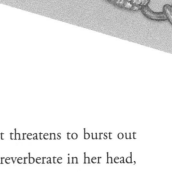

Gabby sits erect. Her pounding heart threatens to burst out of her chest. The thundering beats reverberate in her head, blocking all sound, and her lungs suck in rapid breaths. Her skin is wet, her eyes open wide. The clock glares 2:23 a.m. Noting the familiar curtains and furniture lessens her horror. Gabby hangs her head, allowing her blond hair to tumble over her hands as she covers her face, wiping moisture from her brow. Shivering, she rubs her arms to rid her body of goose bumps. The disturbing images carved into her brain cannot be removed as easily.

She had been campaigning with Richard, and the crowd that had gathered pushed closer. Placing one foot behind another, she had backed away, but the space created instantly filled. Banners blocked her view, and elbows dug into her back. The gap between them grew. Far in the distance, she located his tall frame and dark-brown hair.

She waved her arms and called his name to get his attention, but her actions proved worthless as the noise was deafening. Darkness closed around, collapsing her world—the fear of suffocating rattling. Fighting to breathe, she pushed and elbowed back at the faceless bodies pressing, crushing, and stealing her air. Her sliver of hope to reunite with Richard evolved into a desperate struggle to survive as the monster of fear consumed her body.

Was this nightmare a warning, a sign that she's making a grave mistake?

CHAPTER 2

During the wee morning hours that follow, she tosses and turns in bed as sleep escapes. She should have gotten out of bed hours ago and done something useful instead of wasting time, staring as minutes click by on her bedside clock. Donning her blue silk robe, she pads across the hall and quietly stands in the doorway of her eight-month-old son's room. Matthew is lying on his stomach with his fingers around his favorite toy, a wooden horse carved by Greg, a disabled veteran who works at the horse center. Watching Matthew, his sweet face exuding innocence and perfection, always brings a soft smile to her. Inhaling his scent calms her as though she has meditated, pushing the nightmare into the recesses of her mind.

Of all the mistakes she has made in her life, Matthew is not one of them. Even before he was born, her son became her saving grace, her only reason to live after her husband, Brett, died. They were only married a few months when a bull-riding accident put Brett in a coma, and he never woke up. If she's not careful, these horrific memories resurface to haunt her.

However, now, looking at her baby's brown hair, mouth, and chin, those features resemble a different lover—Richard Wright, the gubernatorial candidate for the state of Texas. No, she's not Mrs. Wright, but she does wear his ring. Yes, it's complicated because few know that Matthew is the candidate's son.

She twirls the emerald-cut diamond surrounded by sapphires adorning her left hand. It's the opposite configuration of the large oval sapphire of the late Princess Di's engagement ring from Charles, the Prince of Wales. Since history records a failed royal marriage, this ring's reverse design will represent the opposite, a marriage that will thrive. After proposing, Richard explained that if he's elected, the public transparency of their relationship will create obstacles much like the royals faced. They need to be aware and prepared.

One week ago, everything in her world seemed right when the handsome, dark-haired man, whose face graces the front cover of most local newspapers daily, got down on one knee and spoke of a future that would launch any girl into a star-studded heaven. His sincerity gleamed, revealing the golden flecks sparkling in his brown eyes. He had spoken of love and a promising future, and she believed that he had changed, moving beyond his playboy reputation.

This Princess Di prototype was not the first ring this couple has exchanged, as they have a history. Four years ago, their relationship soured when Richard cheated. Remorseful after her discovery, he begged for another chance, but she didn't extend forgiveness.

Shortly thereafter, she found true love with Brett Matthews. This once-in-a-lifetime love had compared to those that grace the pages of fairy tales. They fell in love and married. However, unlike the storybook happily ever after ending, Brett left this world, a victim of a traumatic brain injury, leaving behind only memories.

As she centers the engagement ring on her finger, the nostalgia of her painful past dulls the sparkle. However, the past is the past, and for survival, she must move on. To escape those memories, she vowed to start a whole new life.

Richard Wright, the man destined to be the next governor of Texas, a man her father hand-picked and financially backed, is her ticket for change. Her daddy, Wayne King, a wealthy oil and cattle rancher, envisioned a fantastic future for his thirty-one-year-old daughter if she accepted Richard's proposal. His logic seemed like the perfect course of action, and her daddy's wisdom has always faithfully guided her, so she agreed. But this latest nightmare has caused her to question her decision.

But it's not Richard or his career that causes her angst; it's her heart that hides a secret. Daily, she paints on her lipstick smile and follows through with acts that resemble love, but her heart knows it's a lie. Right now, she's trying to help with Richard's political endeavors, hoping that in striving for a mutual goal, love will follow. She did love him once and desperately wants to love him again. So, she takes stock in her daddy's vision and reminds herself that it's best for them to be a family, with Matthew raised by his father.

A few hours later, Gabby inspects her image in her bedroom's large oval mirror. She is wearing a light mint-green chiffon that falls six inches short of her knees, revealing just enough of her shapely leg. Pleased with the look, she completes her outfit with a cream jacket and matching Chanel purse. She's sure to be in the lens of several photographers' cameras on her walk to campaign headquarters. It all comes with the territory as the fiancé of the candidate who leads in the polls. To complete her look, she applies a peachy-orange color to her lips, the perfect tone to compliment her hair and green dress. The doorbell chimes as she tucks a blond hair behind her ear to expose her amethyst earrings, another of Richard's many expensive gifts.

"Miss Gabby, hi!" The perky university graduate student flashes a perfect smile, evidence that her parents invested in braces for their daughter.

"Lola, thank you for being on time."

Despite her circumstances, Lola's positive, contagious attitude won Gabby over during her initial interview. As the girl studies for a master's degree in clinical psychology at the local university, she works several jobs to pay her bills. Gabby was so impressed with Lola's firm commitment to earning her degree that she offered to finance Lola's tuition and housing bill in exchange for childcare. The young woman cried joyful tears before practically knocking Gabby off her feet with a gigantic hug of gratitude.

Lola passes through the entrance, whistling. "Wow, you look fantastic. The press is going to love this outfit. You deserve the entire front page. Mr. Wright made the right choice when he chose you." She smiles at her cleverness in using Richard's campaign slogan as she drops her backpack on the breakfast room chair, then picks up Matthew from his bouncer. "According to the news, his lead over Harold Green is more than 15 percent. Green's too old for office. Gen-Xers want a leader with fresh ideas, something new and different for Texas. My friends talk about Richard. They think he's handsome."

"I'll be sure to tell him that." Gabby straightens the collar of a jacket she's wearing for the first time, acknowledging that her image is now part of Richard's political platform. After Richard proposed, her daddy flew her in the King Air plane to Houston for a shopping spree. She recalls his words. "All eyes will be on you, princess. Richard may be running for office, but it's you they'll be photographing. Never wear the same dress twice." He had then kissed her hand and whispered, "You, my dear daughter, will be the next first lady of this great state. Your mamma would be so proud." With that, he wiped a tear from his eye.

Anna had passed away more than a decade ago. Since then, he married Rita Adams, the lively widow who owns the art gallery where Gabby sells her paintings. Over time working at ArtSmart, the two women developed a good relationship as Rita filled the void left by Anna's death, providing motherly guidance.

As of late, the two women aren't as close as they had once been. Ironically, the widening gap is over a matter of the heart, the elder woman's proclaimed area of expertise. The disagreement is rooted in Gabby's friendship with Stan, the eldest of Rita's two sons.

What's a mother to do when she sees her son wallow in unrequited love? As Rita painfully watched Stan's emotional turmoil, she related everything that had gone wrong in his life to Gabby—his motorcycle accident, rehab stint, and general moodiness. In Rita's opinion, Gabby takes advantage of her son's good nature since he'll do anything she asks. With something as simple as a glance or a touch to his arm, Stan is sucked into Gabby's vortex.

However, Rita appreciates that her thirty-seven-year-old son is striking out to cure his love-sick disease. Recently, he asked Marie, his delightful twenty-four-year-old coworker at the equine center, to be his wife. However, a mother never loses the ability to sense the pain lurking behind her child's eyes. She senses that Marie notices it, too, since she has yet to accept his proposal.

Gabby grabs her Chanel purse and sunglasses from the entry table, then kisses a smiling Matthew, who's happy to be in Lola's arms.

"Bye-bye, my little love. Be a good boy and take your nap so Lola can study. Deal?"

Matthew reaches toward her with his tiny hand.

She kisses it. "Mommy needs to go. See you later."

"Bye, Ms. King. I'll take him for a stroll around the lake. It's such a beautiful fall day."

"Thank you!" she calls over her shoulder. "Phone if you need me."

Lola lifts Matthew's arm as if waving good-bye.

Gabby will walk the eight blocks to campaign headquarters. Since her usual morning jogging routine has been interrupted by reporters and journalists, walking is her only exercise.

Walk whenever possible is the first of many of her daddy's rules she's expected to obey. As she brings the entire set of campaign rules to mind, she hears them in her daddy's deep, commanding voice. *Walk whenever possible—others will recognize you and mention seeing you to friends. Dress fashionably but always conservatively. Everyone who approaches represents his village, thus not one vote, but many. Never seem to be in a hurry, as this can be interpreted as disrespectful and rude. There are no strangers—only friendly voters; make them feel important.*

These are just a few rules in the playbook of do's and don'ts. In addition to the playbook, Gabby gets a daily schedule e-mailed to her by Amanda Jason, the perky, young campaign manager.

She walks at a brisk pace, and squinting in the bright sun, she dons her sunglasses. Thinking she's in for a peaceful trip is a mistake. In a matter of seconds, the clicking of heels indicates a woman is approaching.

"Ms. King, Ms. King, a minute of your time, please? Kristine Walker with local station, KAL."

Gabby pastes on her smile, then turns. "Good morning. Can I help you?" Reluctantly, she takes the business card the reporter is waving in her face. She remembers more of her daddy's words: *Always take the card and let them see you put it in a safe place.*

"Mr. Wright spoke before local museum directors last evening. Do you support his views on the future of the state museum?"

Gabby smiles because her daily morning e-mail anticipated this question and provided her with the proper scripted answer. A man behind a huge projector accompanies the attractive, thirty-something reporter. "We're recording; I hope that's okay?"

"Of course." Gabby removes her sunglasses, shows a flash of white, and then turns a few degrees to capture her best profile before reciting her answer. "Richard Wright understands the value of Texas's rich history and supports the expansion project. The education of our youth is a top priority. Expanding our current museum will provide additional knowledge for students and all citizens and visitors alike."

"Ms. King, on a personal note, have you and Mr. Wright set a date for your wedding?"

This answer is another scripted text she has memorized, but her smile fades. "No, we haven't. Our first and only priority is the election."

"Is it likely your wedding will take place in the governor's mansion and be televised for all Texans? Mr. Wright would be the first Texas governor to marry while in office."

Kristine is not backing down. Is it Gabby's imagination, or is the cameraman closer?

"That's an interesting concept. But as I have answered, the election is our first and only priority." She steps back and replaces her sunglasses. "Thank you for asking. Now, you must excuse me." She nods as instructed, showing her appreciation for the opportunity to engage with the reporter.

Facing the direction of campaign headquarters, she increases her pace. To hell with the rules. Under her dark lenses, she rolls her eyes when she notices the footsteps are still within earshot. *Doesn't Kristine need to get the interview ready for the noonday news? Why is she still following me?*

"Ms. King, just one more quick question about your up-and-coming marriage. In the wake of your husband's death, do you think you will wear white?" With the microphone thrust inches from her face, the question takes her by surprise. "Please, I'm going to be late. After the election, there will be more time for wedding details. Now, excuse me."

"I would love an interview with Senator Wright. Can you put in a good word for me? I've called his office almost daily without results." Her voice trails off with those last words.

Journalism was once a male-dominated job. Women wishing to advance in this chosen career must be exceptional. Gabby recalls her own professional struggles, and her heart softens, feeling some compassion for the reporter's persistence. Extending kindness would be an example of women supporting each other. She makes an about-face in both her attitude and direction, offering her hand. "It's been a pleasure, Kristine. I have your card. I'll check with Richard's manager to get you that interview. Promise."

"Wow, thanks. Really?" Her mouth hangs open as she shakes hands. "Thank you. That would be awesome…really great."

Gabby's laugh is honest. "Kristine, I need my arm back, okay?"

"Oh, sorry. I got carried away." Her face turns red as she pulls her hand away and her shoulders back.

Gabby continues her walk down Congress Avenue, the main street through town, her step a bit higher with satisfaction that she has brightened the reporter's day. Richard's campaign posters adorn most store front windows. *Wright—the Right Choice for Governor* tagline is everywhere. The signs, equal blue and red fields with the word *freedom* written to resemble graffiti, were designed after one of her paintings. She remembers when Richard walked into ArtSmart and purchased her freedom painting. She had thought he was kidding when he told her to take it to the register, but since then, he has focused his campaign on her concept of freedom. It is fun to see her artwork and gratifying to think she's helping his gubernatorial campaign.

CHAPTER 3

The security guard standing outside of campaign headquarters opens the door before Gabby springs up the stairs to greet the stout man with a touch of gray around his temples.

"Beautiful day, Tom."

"That it is, Ms. King. Always a pleasure." His eyes travel from her head to her shoes. "You're a sight for this old man's eyes. Yes, indeed."

She laughs. "Thank you, Tom. Remind me to tell Richard to give you a raise."

"Richard doesn't run the place. Amanda does. Tell her."

"Of course, so silly of me." She bites the inside of her cheek. Whenever Amanda's name is mentioned, her blood boils, and every muscle tenses. She had wanted Richard to fire her, but they were too close to election day to replace the campaign manager. Gabby believes Amanda uses the situation to her advantage and has become increasingly annoying.

Richard's office is on the main floor of a historic building that was once a bank. The floors are light marble, and the dark wooden pillars have intricate carvings. It's a beautiful, historic space, and upon entering, Gabby always feels as though she has been transported back in time. Her freedom artwork posters are displayed on every wall, bringing her back to the present. There are also banners strung from posts, and stickers, pens, and other swag are piled on the counters. Large cardboard boxes are stacked against the wall.

Amanda is quick to notice her arrival.

"Gabby, you're early. Richard is still on his Zoom for at least another ten minutes." Amanda flips her brunette hair to the side and pinches her bright-red lips together.

Gabby offers a forced smile to the ambitious manager. "I'll wait over by the window. You won't even know I'm here." Gabby wonders how the campaign manager types with her long protruding nails, painted to match the color of her lips. She also wonders how Amanda endures wearing those sexy shoes for endless hours.

Amanda follows close behind as her high heels click on the marble floor. Gabby sits on the couch, then turns to face her.

Amanda stands on the step, towering over Gabby with her hands on her hips, exposing more inches of leg beneath her short skirt than any respectable employee. "I'm glad you're here. We need to talk. This game you're playing isn't healthy. It will hurt the campaign."

"I beg your pardon…*game?*" Gabby furrows her brow.

Amanda rubs her chin. "You can drop the act. You put on that innocent face, and some believe you. I'm not one of them, sister. Let's get real…you and me…right now…think you can do that?"

Gabby's eyes are wide, and she sits straighter on the edge of the couch. *What could possibly be the problem? Did she answer some re-*

porter's question off-script? Whatever it is, it must be serious because Amanda's stare is cutting.

"You don't love him. You hate public life. It's only going to get worse. So, take some sound advice—go back to your ranch before you do some real damage."

She's not about to discuss her relationship with Richard. "I don't see how any of this is your business."

"Of course, it's my business. Richard is my business. I've worked too hard to have you destroy everything that has taken years to put in place."

"You're right."

Amanda's eyes double in size at the thought that Gabby agrees because she and Gabby have yet to see eye-to-eye.

"You're right. Your job is getting Richard into the governor's mansion. However, your job does not involve making decisions on his personal life."

"Gabby, don't be so self-righteous and naïve. In six more weeks, the two will be the same."

"Need I remind you that in six more weeks, you'll be out of a job? No campaign, no need for a campaign manager."

"You think I'm just going away? Honestly, I can't sit here and watch this whole sham of a relationship jeopardize his career. He's going to make a great governor. He needs to trust himself and gain confidence. I make him a believer. I'm the woman who has always supported him. Then, your father plants this crazy vision in his mind, and Richard puts that ring on your finger." She rolls her eyes. "I'm the best person to help Richard's career and his personal life. We're great together. We spend time together. He loves me." Amanda stares out the window as if pausing to reload for the next battle. "Open your eyes. You're living your father's dream. He wants you in the governor's mansion. Can't you see it? Wayne King is living vicariously through you, his daughter, and Richard. Richard can't sneeze without King's approval. The two of you are puppets."

In the aftermath of the artillery fire, Gabby stands. "Wow. What makes you think you're right?"

"Gabby, I know I'm right. I know what love looks like. I know what Richard and I have together. I watch you with him, and I'm sorry, sister, but I'm not seeing the love." Her stare is unsettling. "Break it off, now, while there is still time. Little political fallout. The closer to the election, the more votes he'll forfeit. Is that what you want for him? If you cared in the least for Richard and his career, you would cut him loose."

How dare Amanda talk to her like this? The heat inside her chest rises, so she swallows hard, trying to stomp it down. "You're jealous. Words of a scorned woman."

"Richard is so tied up with the election that he's on autopilot when it comes to love, so don't flatter yourself. It will never last." She flits her hand in the air. "By the way, this letter came to the office." Amanda tosses her a white envelope, and it lands on the floor at her feet. Amanda stands firm with her hands on her hips.

Gabby picks up the envelope and holds her tongue as she glances at the unfamiliar return address. Since she doesn't recognize the sender, she tucks it in her purse. She's on defense, and no letter is going to distract her.

Deep in conversation, they ignore the noise that signals the door opening. The large frame of Wayne King enters. Stetson on his head and dressed in a suit, he still turns heads with his crown of white hair.

He rubs his chin, eyeing the two women, who are oblivious to his arrival.

Amanda's face is severe. "Since you're so slow, allow me to spell it out. You don't want him or this life. I love him, and he loves me. What we have is real—very real. I love this life. I have worked hard for all of this." She waves her arms to indicate beyond what's housed within the four walls. "If it weren't for King and his money, Richard wouldn't look in your direction. He was finished with you after you married that…that cowboy." She closes her eyes as if in disgust. "Then, you got pregnant. That's what a desperate woman does to hook a man."

"Amanda," King's deep voice echoes off the walls of the ancient stone building. He approaches. "Get to work. I should fire your ass." His stern tone is like a judge's gavel delivering a death sentence.

Amanda shakes her head and bites her bottom lip. She keenly realizes that their conversation is over, and she glares at Gabby as if to say, *once again, saved by your daddy*.

Waiting to be sure that Amanda is out of earshot, King senses his daughter's tension and holds her in a massive bear hug.

"Hey, princess, don't pay her any mind." He lifts her chin and looks into her sad brown eyes. "What does she know? Richard loves you. He always has. It's good she cares. It makes her better at her job." He pats her back. "Everything will be okay, I promise."

She doubts that his words will come true. Unwilling to meet his gaze, she changes the subject by retrieving the reporter's card and handing it to her daddy. "A reporter…Kristine Walker…I promised her an interview with Richard."

He takes his eyeglasses from his inside coat pocket. "Walker, KAL…this is good publicity." He walks to the desk where Amanda sits and throws her the card. "Amanda, here, do what you're hired to do and set up an interview with this Ms. Walker."

Amanda picks up the card and gives Gabby a chilled stare.

A few seconds later, Richard exits the back office, which served as the vault in the bank's former days. He dons his suit coat. "Sorry, lawyers are tough negotiators. It took longer than I thought to get Field and Field to commit to the corporate-level sponsorship for the museum expansion. This donation is a start, but they could give us twice the amount, and that still wouldn't make a dent in their deep pockets." He joins the twosome, puts his arm around Gabby's waist, and plants a kiss on her cheek. "But mission accomplished because I get to announce the donation at the luncheon today. That should get us several dozen votes." His smile is genuine. He checks his phone for the time. "We need to get going. High-level donors need precious one-on-one face time." With that, he pulls Gabby in closer. "Wow them, darlin,' with your charm."

She lifts her head in search of shared joy over his announcement, and his kiss catches her lips.

She glances at Amanda's desk and smiles with satisfaction that the brunette is watching. That woman has some nerve to ambush her. Gabby is certain that after her daddy's scolding, Amanda knows her place.

King ushers them to the door. "Yes, we should leave. Lunch in twenty minutes."

As they exit, Amanda quickly strides to Richard's side. "Richard, we need to update your schedule. I added a new appointment."

Gabby raises her eyebrows, then looks back to King. He nods his head to signal, *walk with me.* Reluctantly, she falls behind to join him.

Her daddy takes her arm and pats her hand, urging her to relax and reassuring her that all is well.

But is it? Today's confrontation with Amanda triggers increasing self-doubt about her future. The campaign manager dropped obvious clues that she's ready for a fight. Richard and Amanda have hooked up in the past, and his history reveals a weakness for flirtatious women— his biggest flaw in an otherwise decent package. Surely he's aware that any inappropriate behavior will damage his political career. However, she trusts Amanda's words, convinced that the pair have been recently intimate. Her stomach tightens.

This emerging insecurity is like a strangling vine. Even if she can command her heart to genuinely love Richard, will it be enough to keep him from wandering? Love offers no guarantees. Amanda's words torment her, and she's unable to shake them.

Her mind brings up images of Richard with Amanda on the campaign trail a few months ago, smiling with their hands joined. Amanda enjoys the attention. The combination of Amanda's admission of love for Richard and the news that they have been hooking up recently irritates Gabby to her core. Equally bothersome is that the campaign manager knows her secret. Could it be that Amanda's just bluffing to get a reaction, or is it obvious to others that Gabby doesn't love Richard?

Can she fake it for the next four years or possibly eight? She shivers, bringing her nightmare to mind. Is she making a mistake?

CHAPTER 4

The walk to the Texas Museum of History is a short distance from the office. Reporters greet them at the museum's entrance. Gabby steps to the side, watching intently as Amanda takes Richard's arm and steers him toward the local television cameras.

Richard, handsome and confident, answers questions between waving to the crowd and making eye contact with each of them, as if every spectator is his new best friend. He's perfect for political life. By his side, Amanda beams. They proceed through the rotating door.

Gabby is not missed. If she turned around and left, would anyone notice?

As she follows them inside, the museum's atrium lobby bustles with conversation as people gather around circular tables set masterfully with white linens and Texas yellow roses as centerpieces. Gabby recognizes some prominent oilmen and ranchers—most of them her daddy's friends. Directly in front of her stands Governor Johns with his wife, Monica. The governor is deep in conversation with Senator Stevens.

Monica waves. "Hello, Gabby. It's so good to see you."

"Mrs. Johns, it's always a pleasure." She nods. "Thank you for everything you and the governor are doing, especially this luncheon. We appreciate your endorsement."

"It's our way of giving back. We remember our journey. It's exciting and scary at the same time." Monica extends her hand to touch her arm. "You'll be fine, although it might not always seem that way. If you're free next Friday, bring Richard to the mansion, and I'll give you a tour. You can start envisioning your new life there. A quiet evening away from all of this is what you need."

"That's very generous. Thank you." She feels wetness on her upper lip and under her arms as Monica affirms the future. "I'll have Richard's office call you. Please excuse me." She gives a nod of respect before leaving.

Gabby makes brief conversation with others in her path as she meanders to the front of the room in search of Richard. She finds him in conversation with a young man.

When she's within his reach, he smiles as he wraps his arm around her. "Gabby, you remember Bobby Thoman, the museum director."

"Of course. Thank you for this lovely luncheon, Mr. Thoman. Richard and I value your support." Using a firm handshake, she makes eye contact.

Mr. Thoman rubs his hands together. "It's showtime. Shall we?" He leads them to the front table before taking his position at the podium for the welcoming address, followed by Governor Johns, who will introduce Richard.

During his speech, Richard announces Field and Field's donation to help finance the museum expansion program, and the room explodes with applause. Everyone jumps to their feet. Gabby stands and claps with the crowd, but her smile disappears when Amanda appears and positions herself next to Richard. *What is she doing? Shouldn't the campaign manager stay behind the scenes?* The cameras flash.

Gabby's eyes land on her daddy at the adjacent table; however, she's unable to get his attention.

Amanda stands behind Richard for the rest of his speech, and Gabby's blood boils.

CHAPTER 5

The morning paper's front page depicts Richard at the museum luncheon with Amanda, smiling widely in her short skirt and high heels. Gabby covers her mouth, afraid that she will lose her morning coffee. However, she'll have satisfaction in announcing the first lady's invitation to the governor's mansion next Friday evening. She'll bypass the campaign manager and arrange an additional photo session herself. She leans back in her chair, envisioning Richard and her standing arm-in-arm on the famous front staircase and reporter Kristine Walker getting her promised private interview. The following day, Richard Wright will be plastered all over the front page with his fiancée, Gabby King. She twirls the ring on her left hand.

These feelings of jealousy are confusing and in contrast to her heart screaming to escape this madness. Now, she's sparring for position. What's driving this? Is she competing with Amanda for the satisfaction of winning? Or does she really want the job? It's pure craziness with the election next month.

Suddenly she remembers the letter Amanda handed her yesterday that remains unopened in her purse.

She carefully opens the envelope and unfolds the single white page.

> *Ms. King,*
>
> *Due to the lack of response to the letter I sent a few months ago concerning the estate of my brother, Brett Matthews, I arrived in town yesterday. Please accept my invitation to meet at The Foundation Room at noon tomorrow.*
>
> *Respectfully,*
> *Brandon Matthews*

Gabby scratches her head, intrigued since there is no contact information for this man who claims her late husband's last name. She recalls that a certified letter had arrived the day of the spring's primary vote. Her daddy thought it was an opportunist canvasing the obituaries, and she had assumed it was nothing because her daddy never mentioned it again, and her former husband had always claimed he was an only child. Should she give this letter to her daddy? Her curiosity is piqued, and, still in anger mode from the newspaper's front page, she accepts this challenge. What has she got to lose? The noon hour is only three hours away.

The Foundation Room is an exclusive membership-only five-star restaurant, and reservations are hard to get. It doesn't seem like the efforts of a sick fly-by-night get-rich-quick scam. If Mr. Matthews is not a member, who helped him? She rubs her chin before neatly replacing the letter, tucking the envelope back into her purse.

No need to bother Richard or Daddy. Her calendar shows Richard speaking at the country club to the men's group; however, her schedule is open. *Okay, Mr. Matthews, I accept.*

CHAPTER 6

G abby's dress is smart and conservative, and she thinks she'll be less noticeable if she blends in with the suit-and-tie culture of the business lunch crowd. As she walks the few blocks from her condo, no reporters ambush her, and for that, she is grateful. A white-haired gentleman smiles as he opens the door at the street level. It's nice that the good manners of the old days still thrive. She nods and smiles a thank you.

When the elevator door opens to the club's upper-floor restaurant, a male host immediately greets her by name as if he is expecting her arrival and extends his elbow to escort her to her table. The room resembles old Texas with its dark wooden beams and brown leather nail-trimmed chairs. The dining room tables are set with white linens and fine china, and conversation fills the air. The host slows his gait to indicate the window table set for two with the seated man now standing.

Her breath leaves, and her mind swirls as if a funnel has set in, scattering collected photos from her past. Her hand reaches for her chest, she sways, and the man rushes to her side.

"Steady, I'm so sorry," the stranger says, holding her around her waist. "I thought the shock might be perhaps too much, and I can see that my thinking is right."

He towers over her and ushers her to the chair with arms that are firm and muscular. He smells of pine. He's strong, like a redwood in the forest.

"Can I get you anything?"

He must be talking because his mouth is moving, although she's not hearing. Her vision blurs and then darkens, so she holds her head in her hands. Water flows from her eyes. She doesn't dare look at the stranger. *Is he a stranger?* Her body shakes uncontrollably. *Oh my GOD! His wavy brown hair, his nose, his build, the striking resemblance…*

Other diners turn in their chairs, giving them unwanted attention. The man says, "I knew this would be hard. Take some slow, deep breaths. There isn't any way to disguise the likeness." He hands her his handkerchief. "I know it's shocking. It's obvious that you need a minute."

A minute, —this man thinks I need a minute. My husband appears to have come back from the dead—that deserves more than a minute. Gabby, pull yourself together.

She wipes her eyes with the handkerchief and takes a slow, deep breath. She wills herself to speak, although she's unable to glance at his face. "Please sit down. You gave me a fright. Not sure I'll recover." She gives a nervous chuckle.

He reaches across the table for her hand. "Forgive me. It's a long story, and I would love to share it with you." She abruptly pulls her hand away as though his touch would be like reaching into a cold grave.

"This isn't going well. I rehearsed our meeting thousands of times, and never was it this awkward. I've read so much about you that I feel like I know you, but I understand that you don't know me at all." His face softens.

"You got that right." She keeps her eyes lowered. Does he see how her hands tremble? She places them on her lap.

"I'm just going to start talking, okay?" He clears his throat. "Brett didn't know I existed. Our parents didn't know I existed. At the time, they didn't have a nickel to rub together. Our father, the sole bread-winner, was a mere ranch hand. A surprise of twins on delivery day would mean two additional mouths to feed, a tremendous burden for the young couple. So, when I was born, the midwife told them that I didn't make it, that I was a stillbirth." He motions for the approaching waiter to come back later. "The midwife knew of a prominent family desperate for a child. We were born small, less than five pounds each, so a tiny bundle wasn't hard to hide." He pauses and fidgets with the prongs on the fork. "I'm not saying it was the right thing to do; I'm just telling you the facts as I know them."

Finally, Gabby gains the courage to lift her head. She's mesmerized by his profile, which reveals a profound likeness to the man she still loves. Dare she look into his eyes? She squeezes the handkerchief tighter.

Keeping his same tone and pace, he says, "My mother told me this story on her deathbed. That was less than a week after Brett's bull-riding accident. Brett's accident was all over the papers, so she thought I should know the truth."

He turns back to face her. This time she's able to study his features, the likeness uncanny.

"It was a surprise to me then, just like it's a surprise to you now. That was a little over a year ago. I wished desperately to meet my brother. However, since he never regained consciousness, it felt best to let the past be the past."

"But now you feel differently. What changed?" She places a strand of loose hair behind her ear.

"With the loss of my mother, I began thinking about family, about you, and I thought you had the right to know. We haven't been formally introduced." He gives an appreciative grin and holds out his hand. "I'm Brandon—Brandon Matthews. I took my rightful name after my mother passed."

She disregards his extended hand and instead taps her finger on the tablecloth. "What do you want? What are your intentions?"

"To get to know you. With my mother passing, it seems you are the only family I have." He smiles and offers her his hand a second time.

As the words are spoken, the waiter snaps a photo of them with his cell. She startles. Brandon stands to protect them as if her behavior summons danger.

"What is this?" Her wide eyes dodge back and forth. Something isn't right. "I have to get out of here." She searches Brandon's face, a reminder of her loved one who is no longer near, and her pulse races. She dashes across the dining room toward the exit door.

She hurries down the stairs hearing the echo of her steps bouncing off the cement walls, matching the pounding of her heart...another nightmare.

CHAPTER 7

The following day, the newspaper says it all.

CANDIDATE'S FIANCÉE STEPS OUT.

If Richard Wright cannot keep his own house in order, what does that mean for the state of Texas? The accompanying photo shows Brandon with his hand reaching across the table and touching Gabby's hand.

Maybe this is the work of Harold Green's team. High stakes are involved, and the closer they get to the election, the dirtier the campaign strategies become to discredit the opponent. It's a popular tactic. But how did a photographer get this pic? The waiter snapped his photo much later during their conversation. This photo was taken by someone with a long-lens camera much earlier in their meeting. Surely it had been planned. Or was she so upset with the possibility of seeing her husband's ghost that she missed some obvious signs? She rubs her forehead. Is this a chance happening, or was it orchestrated to smear Richard?

If Brandon Matthews played a part in this manipulation to print downright lies, he's some actor. Now, her flaw, her generous ability to think the best of people, looks like ignorance. How could she have been so stupid?

Today, Amanda's words ring true. Maybe Gabby isn't cut out for political life. None of this would have happened if she were back at the ranch. She hangs her head in shame. Brandon is certainly related to Brett, and he did seem sincere. Even so, now that her every move is in the spotlight, she should never have met him alone.

Every *would-have, should-have,* and *could-have* thought bombard her thinking. She's unable to get the pesky voices out of her head. After reexamining the series of events, Richard never meets with a woman alone. He always has Amanda or King when they campaign just for this very reason. Duh, it fits under the most important category—*protect the candidate.* She straightens the ring on her finger. Wearing his ring has saddled her with the same guidelines and restrictions. Yes, she's at fault, but the situation seems contrived.

Gabby's furious. "Brandon Matthews, you snake," she hisses. She picks up her phone. It's still on silent, and there are six missed calls… Richard, her daddy, and four voice messages from Amanda. All before 8:00 a.m.

She listens to one of the messages from a screaming Amanda. "Gabby, call me ASAP. Once again, it's up to me to clean up your mess. Obviously, you weren't thinking. Go back to the ranch where you belong."

The slam of a car door outside, followed by voices, piques her attention. She pulls the kitchen curtain to the side. Three reporters stand on her small lawn, and a van from the local news station is parked across the street. *Those vultures.* If she hides inside, is that giving validity to their lies? Can she pull off a candid interview explaining her innocence? She doubts if she can make matters worse.

Matthew cries. This can wait.

Gabby walls up in her condo as if she's in quarantine. The purposeful acts of taking care of her son dampen her anger and provide distance from her problem. She bites her lip as she waits for her daddy to answer. The phone rings twice before he picks up. She braces to face the consequences and learn about the damage to the campaign.

The weight of blame crushes her as if she's trapped under a heavy boulder, preventing her from taking a needed breath. Only her admission of poor judgment will remove it.

"I'm so sorry. I never thought…"

"Start from the beginning." She's heard his business-like tone before, but she has never been the one on the opposite side.

"I never thought…"

King is not one for small talk in damage control mode. "Just give me the facts."

"Amanda handed me a letter from a Brandon Matthews, the same man who sent that certified letter disputing Brett's estate. Do you remember?"

"Yes, I tossed it. Fortune seekers, combing through obituaries. It's disgusting."

"The letter asked me to meet him for lunch at The Foundation Room. I thought I should hear what he had to say."

"You didn't think to run this by Richard or your old man?"

She can hear the disapproval in his voice. "The Foundation Room is for members only. I thought it would be safe. I'm sorry, really sorry."

"It's too late for that. We're dealing with the fallout."

"Daddy, did you look at the photo? The man, Brandon Matthews, is the spitting image of Brett."

Silence.

"He said that he's Brett's twin. I believe him. Daddy, did you see the picture?" She bites her nail.

"Princess, I'm looking for my magnifying glass. You know my eyes aren't as good as they used to be. My ears must be failing too. Did I hear you right?" He clears his throat. "He said he was Brett's twin? These folks are sick. The nerve, using grief to scam for money."

"The likeness is remarkable. It was weird, so strange. It was as if Brett was on the other side of the table. I thought I was losing my mind."

"What…you don't say? Hold on."

She hears rummaging and imagines him searching through the desk drawers.

"I'll be dammed. He does look like Brett. Interesting. I was so enraged by the article that I missed the resemblance."

"One thing I don't understand though…if Brandon wished to introduce himself, why would he let Harold Green use this to discredit Richard? Why would he want to hurt us?"

"Good question and an important one to figure out." There's a pause. "I didn't see this one coming. Hey, princess, hold on a minute."

She's certain he muted his phone because there is a long pause.

"We're ready. Start over and be as exact as you can."

"Yes, Daddy." She feels like she's twelve and being asked to explain a bad math test grade.

"Princess, you're on speaker. Richard and Amanda are here. Give us every detail."

She pauses to gather her thoughts since she wishes to recall the events leading up to that day and to retell Brandon's story exactly.

Without interruptions during her recital, she suspects her version of the fiasco at the restaurant is being recorded.

After she finishes, no additional questions or comments are voiced, which is odd. She had hoped she would be included in the brainstorming of a fix. Instead, after an abrupt disconnection, she feels alone and isolated. She can only imagine the conversation the three of them are having at her expense.

The call leaves her exhausted; her morning coffee sits cold, and Matthew's taking his midmorning nap. Peering out the window, careful not to be noticed, she sees only one reporter still camped out in her front yard, a reminder that she forgot to ask the team for guidance on handling them. The young reporter appears to be reading a novel. Perhaps, he'll get bored or get called away on another assignment.

CHAPTER 8

King Ranch

Driving the two hours from the city provided Gabby with much-needed mental clarity. During the drive, she called Ella, Stan's brother's wife. She and Ella were sorority sisters and continue to maintain a close relationship, even though Ella moved to Washington, D.C., with Will two years ago. Disappointed that her best friend didn't answer, she left a voice message. Ella tends to find humor in the worst of life's events and reminds Gabby to take things less seriously. Disturbing events like the one today emphasize how much Gabby misses these girlfriend chats.

Gabby opens the main gate into the ranch and releases a sigh. It feels good to be home. As she takes a deep breath of country air, she realizes how much she has missed open spaces. She imagines riding her horse through the meadows, crossing creeks lined with trees, and hearing the soothing sounds of cattle grazing in the pastures.

The King Ranch covers three hundred thousand acres. Her mother's ancestors first took possession of the land northeast of the city, but Wayne King had the wisdom to expand its borders. After success drilling for oil on a newly purchased parcel, the King name was magnified throughout the region.

Fifty years ago, the young, ambitious King was passing through on business when he met the shy, mysterious Anna. Prior to their meeting, the handsome stranger courted many ladies during his travels. After completing his business deals, he would continue to the next town, leaving them behind in his dust. However, this time he was smitten. Wooing Anna involved convincing her father that he would honor their family values. Early in their courtship, it became clear that Anna loved the land, and her feet had grown deep roots. After Cupid's arrow pierced King's heart, the price of Anna's love included this cherished land. When King wed Anna, his life changed three-hundred and sixty degrees.

Gabby places her hand over her chest as her eyes feast on the sights surrounding her. The main house, barn, and bunkhouse, built by her grandparents, are clustered together. Then her eyes follow a few hundred yards down the dirt lane, where her house sits to the right, across from the lake, and in the opposite direction is Stan's house, its construction finished just last year.

The soothing pleasure of home seeps deeper into her soul. As she takes another deep breath, her worries and anxieties now seem minuscule compared to earlier.

The pride that wells up inside when she's here confirms her belief that she's a part of the land. Did she inherit her mother's genes? This mission to change her destiny, to escape the ghost of Brett's death by leaving the ranch, has been challenging. Now, it seems as if his ghost has found her instead. Is she chasing after a dream that doesn't align with her purpose? Is this another omen? The bang of the screen door, followed by footsteps, interrupts her thoughts.

"Oh, my child, I've waited weeks to get my hands on your little one." Jamie claps her hands as she peers through the car window at the sleeping baby.

Jamie and Rusty are considered family. King hired Rusty as his ranch foreman four decades ago. His wife, Jamie, started as the cook for the ranch hands, especially those who call the bunkhouse home during the week. After Gabby's mother, Anna, died twelve years ago, King moved Rusty and Jamie into the main house. The couple was never blessed with children, so the arrangement worked well for both parties; it made their families whole. The housekeeper, who has also been the cook for many years, has proven trustworthy, and Gabby values her opinion more than Rita's.

Gabby runs around the car and embraces the older plump white-haired woman. She rocks her back and forth, inhaling the aroma of recently baked bread that lingers on Jamie, and craves the safe-haven warmth of her bosom and encircling arms. Indeed, she is home.

"Oh, Jamie, I've missed you and all of this." She releases her arms to wipe the tears.

Jamie, wise beyond measure, holds Gabby at arms-length and studies her face. "We'll have time to talk later. Let's get Matthew into the house, and then we'll have iced tea. I picked fresh mint this morning."

She releases the seat belt to remove the car seat, and Jamie throws the diaper bag over her shoulder. The rest of the luggage can wait. Jamie places her arm around Gabby's shoulder and escorts her up the wooden stairs and through the front door. In addition to being taken under Jamie's wing, the familiarity of the house provides further comfort to settle her edgy spirit.

For the first time since her nightmare, there is reassurance that everything will be okay. She should have come back to her roots sooner. The feeling that she had to escape the ranch to change the direction of her life seems to have dissipated after the past week's events.

Her phone vibrates. Richard's face appears on the screen.

"Hey, where are you?"

"At the ranch. I just got here."

"I thought you might be going there, but I wasn't aware that you'd decided. It doesn't matter. I need you here. If you leave now, you'll be back with time to spare. We got an invitation to the concert opening the F1 races. After your botched photo with this strange man plastered all over *The Statesman*, we need to squash the rumors about our quote-on-quote "unstable" relationship. We must be seen together. This is the perfect opportunity. I already sent an RSVP."

"Richard, I can't do that. I just got here."

"Turn around, come back. Jamie will watch Matthew. I'll send a sitter. If I put her in a car now, she'll be there in two hours. Surely, Jamie can watch him until she arrives."

"Richard…"

"Don't *Richard* me. Get on board, Gabby. You created this mess, so you need to stretch yourself a little to clean it up. Wear something nice…sexy."

"Where are we going?"

The phone is silent. He's disconnected.

She bites her cheek, and her blood pressure rises. She punches in her daddy's number.

"Hey, Daddy." She inhales, preparing to voice her case.

"Princess, make it quick."

"I'm at the ranch. Got here about ten minutes ago. Richard called. What do you think? Do I need to drive back to town?"

"Yep, sorry, princess. You should be on his arm."

"But, Daddy, I—"

"Can't be helped. The people of Texas want a romance, not some fractured infidelity. But more than that, they want a man who's in charge. A man in whom they have confidence, who can keep his house in order. That photo in the paper got more attention and comments than any other. Folks love this stuff. If Green was behind this, it's going to backfire." King chuckles. "Princess, get your butt back here and play like you and Richard are anchored together, unsinkable. We'll show the Green team who the Wright team is."

Grudgingly, she knows he's spot-on about the mess she created. She rubs her neck. So much for calming her edgy spirit with ranch time and falling asleep tonight, the open window letting in a light breeze, the soothing sound of the babbling creek lulling her to sleep. She'll drive back to do this, vowing this will be the last time.

A few minutes later, after giving instructions to Jamie on Matthew's care, the front door opens, and Stan, her stepbrother by marriage, appears. His Stetson hat in his hands exposes a sunburned forehead, the area enhanced by a receding hairline. Ryder, his borador companion, stands by his side.

"Welcome back. I can't wait to see how much Matthew has grown." He's all smiles. He kisses her cheek, embraces her with his strong arms, lifts her, and swings her in circles. He smells of sweat, but she doesn't mind. His genuine happiness to see her overrides his stench from horseback riding with the cattle. Ryder loops around them, hoping to be included in their game.

She giggles. "Put me down. You're going to break your back. You're not young anymore."

"Never. You calling me old?" His eyes twinkle. "Where's the little guy?" He searches the room.

"Sleeping upstairs in his crib." She reaches down to give attention to Ryder.

He gives Jamie a nod accompanied by a smile. "Something smells good. What's for dinner?"

"Your favorite—pot roast." Jamie's quick to answer.

"You're an angel. Too bad Rusty got you first." He grabs a chocolate cookie from the large ceramic vessel shaped like a pig before facing Gabby. "How long are you staying?"

"Unfortunately, I've been summoned by Daddy to drive back to town immediately for a PR photo." Aware of Stan's dislike for Richard, she purposely avoids mentioning his name.

Stan's face drops the smile. "Too bad. Tonight, I'm setting up the telescope for stargazing. Jamie has never seen the Canis Major Dwarf Galaxy. The viewing will be perfect because the moon is new."

She pouts. "I would love to stargaze. Raincheck?"

"Can't make a promise that it will be as spectacular." He nods to Jamie. "Thanks for the cookies. I'll be back for dinner."

Jamie pats him on his backside. "You better be back. I made it especially for you."

Stan nods, places his black Stetson on his head, and exits. His limp, a souvenir from a motorcycle accident a few years ago, is more prominent than when he arrived.

CHAPTER 9

A t campaign headquarters, Amanda raises her eyes and then returns to her computer without acknowledging Gabby's arrival. *Would it be too much for her to say hello?* She makes a path between a pile of cardboard boxes that have recently arrived. Richard is conversing with another man in his office, so she'll remain in the main room.

Even though she's dressed for the evening in a dark-blue silk dress with a sweetheart neckline and high heels, she grabs a boxcutter from a nearby counter and tackles the stack, opting to be useful rather than be under Amanda's scrutiny while she waits.

The first box she opens has hundreds of red, white, and blue balloons. These must be for the celebration party on election night. She labels the box with a Sharpie before carrying it to the closet. Upon opening the second box, she breaks a nail and curses under her breath. Inside are thousands of "Wright is the Right Choice" campaign buttons. She picks one up and turns it over in her hand, digesting the words. *Is he the right choice for me?*

Her thoughts are interrupted by the security guard opening the door to assist a delivery man who balances a large floral arrangement.

"Wow, these are beautiful. Thank you." Amanda signs his form, then tips the man. She opens the card. "Gabby, these are for you."

"For me, from whom?"

"Your new love interest." Amanda laughs, flipping the card from her fingers. It hits the corner but bounces back, landing on the desk. "Try to keep this out of the papers. Take these away. How am I supposed to work with all of this clutter?"

Gabby retrieves the card, then lifts the vase from Amanda's desk and places it on the coffee table.

The card, written in impeccable penmanship, reads:

> *Gabriella,*
> *I'm sorry. Please call me.*
> *Brandon Matthews*

She buries her nose in the bouquet of pink roses, white chrysanthemums, and fragrant stargazer lilies. *Does he know that pink roses are her favorite?* Her gut believes Brandon should be given a chance to explain. However, how to handle this matter is out of her control. Still in damage control from their meeting at the Foundation Room, the campaign team will handle all future interactions.

Voices get louder, and seconds later, the men exit the back office.

"Gabby, always a pleasure. I'm looking forward to our evening." Steven Prime, CEO of the biggest tech company in the city and an important donor and supporter of Richard, reaches for her hand, then leans in for a fatherly kiss on her cheek. The older man has done this on every occasion they've met, so she's prepared.

"Mr. Prime, what a delightful surprise."

"Please, drop that Mister stuff. We're friends. Mr. Prime is the name used by my enemies." He gives a robust laugh, and Gabby is certain his belly rolls, visible from his unbuttoned suit coat.

He waves his finger in the air. "Richard, you kept my invitation a secret."

"I wanted to give you the pleasure," Richard says.

Prime turns to face Gabby. "You're my guests at the F1 track." He claps his hands. "I'm hosting the Mercedes racing team. We'll start with a cocktail hour to meet the team, then dinner, a concert, dancing, and then the best thrill of all." His voice is animated, and his eyes sparkle. He's as giddy as a kid going to the amusement park. "Well…"

"Well, what?" Gabby shifts her eyes and looks to Richard for guidance.

"Ask me about the thrill." His impatience makes it obvious he's about to burst. "The team will take you for a ride on the track."

"Really?"

"Isn't that exciting? Imagine the adrenaline rush, the speed going into the turns. It's my special gift. Unfortunately, my doctor advises that I not ride due to my heart. But you young folks can have all the fun."

CHAPTER 10

I never thought of car racing as a team sport. Tell me more." Gabby takes a sip of her wine, intrigued by the thirty-seven-year-old driver. She's never been interested in the sport that came to the city a few years ago after the track was built.

"Our team has four drivers for our two cars and a few dozen members in the pit crew." Lee Hamilton, the driver, motions to a group of men standing near the stage. "Then, behind the scenes are about a hundred others."

His sleeve creeps up his arm as he points. She recognizes the large black dial of his watch as the popular Pilot's Watch from the International Watch Company. Upon entering the circuit track, she saw the company's banner draping the front gate. "See that trophy?" He points to the gleaming silver and gold vessel. "It's the coveted prize, the Championship Trophy made by Fox Silver. The driver's names since 1950 are engraved up the spiral, but the trophy is the team's trophy. No man earns it by himself." He chuckles. "I like the idea that

I take part in the winning. Notice, our team is listed for last year's race." He stands tall, and she doesn't blame him for being proud. It's nice to see.

Steven Prime's invitation to this fascinating venue has melted her earlier rage at Richard's request to return to the city. The concepts of speed, engineering, and mechanics that car racing offers are outside her realm of knowledge. Her conversations this evening have been an exchange of questions and answers since she has much to learn.

Wishing to keep their conversation moving, she lifts her chin to read his face. "Do you love it?"

"I love the way driving makes me feel. When you drive, you're completely committed…total concentration, pure adrenal rush, all faculties on high alert…nothing else matters. You are one with the car. One could say…together, the driver and the car *are* the machine." He takes a sip of his soda. "The travel, living in hotel rooms, not so much."

She notes a slight sadness in his voice. "You have time off in the off-season."

"The off-season is working time."

She runs her finger around the lip of the glass. "You'll need to explain."

"Race car driving is a misunderstood sport. To race, I need to keep this body mentally and physically fit." He grabs his bicep. "I'm in the gym every day lifting weights, and sparring with my boxing partner helps sharpen my reflexes. Then, there's time with the simulator. That's where I get to push my skills to the limit without wrecking the car or killing myself." He searches her face as if anticipating shock at this realization. "You should come, watch, and learn. Car racing needs a voice in this town, especially from someone who may be the next first lady."

He finishes the last ounce of his drink and crushes the can. "On that note, let's go. I understand that we're taking you for a lap or two. Ready?"

She backs away from the captivating stranger. "I don't think that's such a good idea."

"And why not?" He steps closer. His nearness raises the hair on her arms.

"You'll like it. I promise. It will be one of the most exciting things you've ever done." He takes the glass from her hand, places it on the nearby table, and leads her by the elbow. "Time to give you your first taste of the racing experience. We modified a car to give potential investors an understanding of the sport."

Her foot drags.

"Mr. Prime's request. Never disappoint a key investor. I could throw you over my shoulder." His laugh is robust. "Let's go tell him and that guy you're with...what's his name...yes, Wright, to head to the grandstand to watch the show."

She holds her stomach and shakes her head.

"You'll be fine. Trust me. We aren't going full speed, promise." He nods at Prime, then ushers her out the door toward the track. Cars are already in the pit, and she smells a greasy mixture of oil and gasoline. There are mechanics in one-piece jumpsuits. She recognizes two of them from the party. They give Hamilton the okay sign, and he waves back. She feels reassured when she sees another guest getting out of the racing gear. He's still standing; how bad can one lap be, right?

Hamilton holds a leather jacket and motions for her to put her arm in the sleeve. "This should fit." His eyes drop to her cleavage as he zips up the jacket, his fingers nearly touching her.

Heat rises to the top of her head. Should she be upset or pleased that he noticed?

He turns, grabs a helmet, and places it on her head. "This may be slightly too big. Lift your head." He pulls the strap tight under her chin, then looks at her through the plexiglass face protector.

He's treating her like a child, and she rolls her eyes.

He smiles. "That should do it," he says and taps the top of the helmet.

A photographer arrives and shoots a few photos. Then Gabby turns and forces a wave to Prime and Richard, who make their way to seats in the grandstand.

A second driver approaches, and Hamilton gives him the thumbs-up sign. The man hops into the car behind the steering wheel. The car, white with a large blue strip down the middle with a blue number six-ty-one on the side, rides low to the ground. "Ready?" Hamilton lifts her as if she's weightless over the car's frame into the confined space. In disbelief, she turns to him. "You're not driving?"

"Nope, not this time. My friend gets the pleasure." He winks.

Noticing that her short dress has ridden up, exposing more of her thigh, she's helpless to adjust it in the tight space. Her mind whirls, and she startles as Hamilton reaches over her to buckle the seat belt. From this intimate act, one would get the impression that they were familiar friends, giving fuel for more outrageous speculation from the press.

She is practically seated in the driver's lap. After the click of the belt, Hamilton tells the driver, "She's ready." He winks, then slaps the hood of the car. Immediately, the engine roars, the car accelerates, and

Gabby turns to watch Hamilton standing with his hand on his hips and a grin on his face as the car rolls toward the track's first turn.

This is far more than what she had bargained for. She enjoys riding Lady, her mare, at full gallop, but that's a different scenario from this race car. From the questions she asked this evening, she's aware that a lap is almost three and one-half miles, which takes around a minute and a half at the regular speed. Perhaps if she closes her eyes and focuses on her breathing, the time will pass quickly. She can do this.

Who is this driver? Wanting to know the name of the man who could send her to her death, she tries to communicate; however, the engine is loud, and with these helmets, he can't hear her speaking. Even if he could, she's certain that if he did answer, she wouldn't be able to hear him over the roar. Besides, he hasn't even turned toward her or acknowledged that she's in the car, even though they are pressed against each other.

Seconds later, his hand grabs the gear shift pulling it down, the car accelerates, and then they gain more speed moving into the first turn. She survives that turn, but already, she's sure the speed is over one hundred miles per hour because the scenery whizzes by in a blur. Her heart beats faster, and tension sets in as she braces, pressing her feet into the floorboard. Where should she put her hands?

She remembers her meditation exercises and now is the perfect time to use them. She inhales a long deep breath, but then the car jerks as it shifts gears, followed by what seems to be a sharp turn. Her body stiffens, and she palms the door frame to keep from bumping into the driver's arm. Did he exaggerate that movement to unsettle her?

He turns his head slightly toward her. She wants to see his face, but the safety shield only mirrors her reflection. Her back presses tight into the seat as the driver shifts several gears in seconds. The force molds her into the seat. Their speed must be close to 200 mph. Her world condenses as she focuses on the dash directly before her and no longer lifts her eyes to peer out the windshield. It's too frightening, and her stomach rolls.

She's a bit lightheaded; however, she refuses to give him the satisfaction of reporting that she fainted. She'll complete the lap with grace and honor. Less than another thirty seconds later, the grandstand comes into view. *Thank God, this ride is over. But is it?*

They make the first turn again. *OMG!* She closes her eyes as she is forced into enduring a second lap. Wait, is it her imagination, or is the car slowing down? Opening her eyes, she can make out trees and viewing areas. They're coming to a stop. What once seemed like the engine's roar is now a purr.

The driver bumps her with his elbow as he removes his gloves before turning to remove her helmet. Should she be angry or relieved? Her blond hair cascades, and it's damp from perspiration. She must look a mess to this stranger, but at least she's still alive. Next, he removes his helmet, and his wide smile shows pleasure.

"Brandon Matthews! You could have killed me."

"Nope, hardly. We never slid. We can go faster, but you might wet your panties." He laughs. "You have no color in your face. Take some slow breaths."

She's embarrassed and nervous.

He chuckles again. "I have your full attention, right?"

She'd love nothing more than to wipe the smirk off his face. But she's speechless, afraid that the tears will fall if she opens her mouth to voice her concerns. No act of meditation will calm her fast-beating heart.

"There's no place to run. No photographers. Just you and me."

She turns her head away. He has certainly gotten her attention.

"I didn't think you would meet with me. So, I got creative when I learned that you would be here tonight." He touches her shoulder. "Please don't be mad."

He's got some nerve. "Was Hamilton in on this?" She searches for an answer.

"Maybe..." He hesitates, then says, "Of course." He puts his hands back on the steering wheel. We work together. I'm an engineer on the team. That's why I'm in town."

His eyes show compassion, and his voice empathy. "Let me explain. At The Foundation Room, I didn't know the press would find us—never thought about it. You must believe me. I'm not out to hurt you or Richard Wright. I think it's awful how the press slanted our luncheon date."

He looks sincere. *Is he playing me?* "What do you want from me?"

"As I explained, we're family. I would like to get to know my sister-in-law."

"You have one hell of a way of going about it." She rubs her forehead. Does he notice her hand trembling?

"I'm sorry. The other day...I had no idea, but I learned from that, which is why I'm talking with you here. Just me and you." He looks as if he expects her to praise him.

"Okay, let's take it slow. First, I'm going to be completely honest."

"I would expect nothing less."

She exhales before proceeding, trying to regain her composure. "It's hard. I feel like I'm looking at a ghost. Can you imagine?"

"I've studied Brett's photos online. There is a strong resemblance. We are fraternal twins, not identical. My eyes are brown, not green. If you gave me a chance, you would find several more physical differences. However, our upbringing and backgrounds are completely unalike. I'm reaching out for a relationship with my family."

"You trick me into meeting with you. Then, before asking me to forgive you for making my life a living hell, you scare me to near death. I feel like I've been kidnapped." Her voice quivers.

His smile disappears. "I'm sorry if I upset you. I thought it would be fun."

"Your idea of fun and mine are very different." She lowers her eyes.

"You must admit that racing is exhilarating. I hope you'll forgive me. I never meant to frighten you." His look tells her that he is waiting for her to acknowledge his apology.

"Truthfully, I didn't know what to expect." She clears her throat. "It's like a rollercoaster ride."

He holds her helmet. "Let me help you with this. Think about what I said. We've got to get back before they come looking for us."

She helplessly allows him to fasten the strap, careful not to make eye contact. She has a million questions that need answers. Can she trust this stranger? Surely, there is more to his story.

He guns the engine before shifting the car into gear, then, with a reduced speed, finishes the lap. The pit crew members meet them on their return. Brandon jumps out of the car and explains some mechanical jargon that's totally foreign to her ears. Immediately, he and two others bury their heads under the car's hood. A third team member assists her out of the low seat, and she wobbles before finding her legs.

Prime and King rush to her side.

"We were worried until Hamilton relayed the news about the engine malfunction," Prime says. "Better to troubleshoot now than during the actual race. How was it?"

Gabby removes her helmet and forces the expected smile. "That's a ride I'll never forget."

Prime beams. His chest expands, proud as a peacock.

Her daddy places his arms around her. "You need to tell me all about it. Your fastest speed on the stretch clocked 186 miles per hour. Amazing, maybe I need to invest in this racing stuff." He chuckles.

Gabby searches the grandstand. "Where's Richard?"

"He and Amanda went for an interview with a local news team. Come along." King nudges her. As she's leaving, she turns to see Brandon look up and give her a nod.

Is this mysterious man who he claims to be? Can I survive any more of his fun antics? Her hands are still shaking.

CHAPTER 11

G abby disregards the rules and takes an Uber to campaign headquarters. She's waited ten days for this evening and wants to look perfect. No one would expect her to walk eight blocks in her Jimmy Choo shoes with their five-inch spike heels. Besides, the hot late-afternoon temperature reinforces her attitude that rules aren't laws but mere guidelines.

She shifts the bouquet of daisies, which are beginning to wilt in the heat, from one arm to the other. Her outfit, a dark-purple pencil skirt with a stylish matching jacket, will complement Richard's navy suit.

Tonight is the scheduled interview with Kristine Walker on the steps of the governor's mansion. The broadcast will air live on the evening news, as well as a photo and full article on *The Statesman's* front page tomorrow. At the end of the interview, the governor and his wife will welcome them into the mansion, foreshadowing the anticipated change of residency after Richard is voted in as governor—that is, if the projected poll results hold for the next few weeks. The whole team is excited.

As she climbs the steps to the campaign office, she notices that Tom isn't there to open the door. His shift must be over for the day. However, once inside, the room buzzes with a mix of conversations as political science majors from the college volunteer on the campaign for college credit or community service hours. They fold flyers to be distributed on street corners and in front of popular restaurants. Others man the half-dozen computer terminals working social media websites, their fingers quickly clicking. The busyness of the headquarters has increased these last few weeks because the finish line is in view.

King's wife crosses the room to greet her. "Hello, Gabby," Rita says as she comes over to hug her. "It's been too long."

Gabby has trouble calling Rita her stepmother since she was her boss at the art gallery before introducing her to King.

"Our paths haven't been crossing much. It's been a hectic schedule. You should come over and visit with Matthew."

Rita holds her at arms-length. "I would like that. You're right; I need a good visit with my grandson."

Gabby wipes her brow. "It's days like today that I don't know what I would do without Lola. She's the best, and Matthew adores her. I've been so busy. One would think that I was running for governor as well."

"In a sense, you are. Prepare yourself. This pace will be the norm if our dream comes true." Rita presses her hands together, and her eyes sparkle.

Gabby's face pales. *Dream…isn't a dream supposed to be something to aspire to, not dread?*

"Howdy, princess." King reaches for his daughter. "Big night, to-night."

He's dressed in a suit. She shifts her gaze back to a well-dressed Rita and bites her cheek.

Her daddy puts his arm around her shoulders. "These youngins have interesting points of view." He points to the students gathered around the table. "Fascinating. This old man has learned a thing or two this afternoon." He chuckles. "Hey, we're coming with you. I made a few calls, and the Johns extended us an invite."

"That's great." Her voice squeaks.

Her daddy has coveted this highest position of power in Texas for as long as she can remember. She knows from witnessing his lengthy conversations with his business partners that he regrets not pursuing his own political ambitions. But in his younger days, he was consumed by making the ranch profitable with the cattle trade as he searched for oil. Back then, locals had thought him foolish. He wasn't deterred even though the years weren't kind, and he continued drilling for the precious oil through the setbacks. He acquired massive loans to replace broken drill bits as they probed deeper into the earth's crust until that glorious day when the Texas gold finally sprayed out of the ground. However, the victory was soon overshadowed by Anna's cancer diagnosis. Her life ended quickly, and with it, King's political dreams.

Love wells up from her heart, putting a spontaneous smile on her face as she notices the joy exuding from the older man. His wrinkled lines speak of hard work, commitment, and a realization that his time is short. She's never reflected on what life has in store after he passes. She has always thought him immortal. Today, her eyes tell her that he is not. Not ready to face that, her heart sinks, and she turns away.

Rita has motherly instincts. "Gabby, are you feeling okay?"

Thinking fast, she says, "Sorry, I was pondering tomorrow's schedule. Where's Richard?"

"Richard and Amanda are meeting with a caterer. I don't remember for which event."

"This afternoon? He knows the importance of this interview." She checks her phone for the time. "One would think Amanda could do that on her own." *Meeting with a caterer? You've got to be kidding.*

The Greek-Revival style mansion was constructed in 1854 and has been the home of every Texas governor. It sits in the heart of downtown with a view of the capitol from the second-story balcony, a reminder of just how essential the governor's position is. The walk to the mansion from campaign headquarters is a short few blocks.

After arriving, the foursome gathers on the sidewalk in front of the mansion near the stairs. Kristine Walker and her crew are setting up. It's 6:00 p.m., and the sun is to their backs, so the cameraman will adjust and shoot from an angle.

Kristine wears a navy suit, waves as they approach, and then scurries toward them. "Senator Wright, thank you so much for allowing this interview." Then she turns to Gabby. "Ms. King, it's nice to see you again. I'm appreciative of your efforts to make this happen. I'm excited for the opportunity. I can't thank you enough."

Richard extends his hand. "The privilege is ours. Please allow me to introduce you to Gabby's father, Wayne King, and his wife, Rita.

"Yes, Mr. King, I've read many articles. It's a pleasure. When we get the signal, I'll have you and your wife stand behind Senator

Wright. Ms. King, please stand close to Senator Wright so we can get all of you in the camera lens.

The group positions on the steps as directed, making minor adjustments until the cameraman signals with a thumbs-up.

Kristine approaches Gabby and switches the flowers from her left hand to the right, then winks. "That engagement ring needs to be in full view. Let it shine."

As Richard leans into Gabby and squeezes her waist, Gabby's smile disappears. Does she detect a familiar spicy fragrance?

In front of them, an assistant who has joined the crew counts… "three, two, one," and the red flashing light indicates it's showtime. Gabby's smile could win an Academy Award.

CHAPTER 12

During breakfast the next morning, Gabby Googles the 2008 fire that prompted extensive renovations to the governor's residence. The articles she found noted that caution prevailed in restoring the original architectural design and decor as accurately as possible.

She takes a sip of coffee and leans back in her chair to reflect on the tour that Monica Johns graciously provided last night. Monica stated that the tour's purpose was to help them adjust and lessen anxiety about the place they will call home if the predictions of a Richard Wright victory hold true.

But instead of reassurance, the antique mirrors, dark wooden furniture, heavy floor-length drapes, and ornate chairs offered a sense of dread and darkness that matched Gabby's mood, causing her to sink deeper into despair.

She'll ask Richard's opinion when he comes to breakfast after showering, hoping his enthusiastic opinion will unburden her troubled spirit. *Can I live with the marble bust of Sam Houston for four years?* Recalling the sculpture's expression makes her giggle since the artisan made the hero look like he had just seen a ghost. The mansion's old and dark ambiance supports the rumors that it's haunted.

Seriously though, it's not only her future she has to consider, but how will little Matthew fare if they live there? He'll be restricted to the private quarters on the upper level most of the time. In contrast to the dark furnishings on the main level, she'll decorate those rooms with bright colors and open the drapes. However, she remembers Monica's warning about the intense security lights that illuminate the capital building at night and stream through the mansion's windows. Last evening Monica made her point by opening the drapes, allowing Gabby to witness the unwelcome light invading the private space.

Her thoughts are interrupted by Matthew's cry.

She rescues him from his crib. "Good morning, my little man." She knocks on the bathroom door. "Richard?"

He opens the door. "What? I'm running late."

"Matthew requested to have breakfast with his dad."

"Not happening. I have a 7:30 with the men's group at the Presbyterian Church."

She pouts. "That isn't on my schedule."

"Amanda added it yesterday." He finishes combing his hair.

"Is Amanda going to be there?"

"I said it's a men's group. I don't have time for your insecurity." He throws the towel over his shoulder and pushes past her.

She follows him into the bedroom. "Will you be home tonight? It's been ages since we've had family time with just the three of us."

"I don't have time for this, Gabby. No, I won't be home tonight. I got an invite to the college tennis match. They want me to warm up with the team. It will be great public relations. Youths made up 30 percent of voters in the last election." He finishes buttoning his shirt.

"Pack my gym bag with a tennis outfit—all white. I can't clash with school colors. Get those new sneakers."

She does as she's told, carrying Matthew on her hip while she performs the task.

He dons his suit coat over his shirt. A loose tie drapes around his neck, and he grabs the gym bag, then turns to retrieve his keys off the dresser.

"What about your tennis racquet?"

"Wilson donated a dozen. I'll use one of those and give the rest to the team. Got to run."

He opens the door to find a handful of reporters waiting. He turns, flashes a smile, and waves before she hears him give the crowd that has gathered on their lawn a loud, cheery, "Good morning!"

She peeks through a crack in the kitchen curtain. The night security guard holds the reporters back at a distance as Richard climbs into a black limo. The vehicle's windows are tinted, so she's unable to see if Amanda is in the car. Now, recent security precautions have expanded to include Gabby's downtown townhome. The violence in other states during elections has led to increased safety measures.

Her hopes of getting some reassurance from Richard about last night are dashed. Instead, she feels insignificant with his demands that lack kindness, much less any sign of love. The press outside gets a better greeting. She feels like she's already in a marriage that has gone bad. Was their exchange this morning a foretelling of the future? Should she have faith that this is temporary, or is that thinking naïve? If Richard wins the election, will Texas be his bride?

Gabby reaches for the trinity knot charm on her necklace and moves it back and forth on its chain. It's a nervous habit that has been part of her life for over a decade, and she's never tried to quit. Her mother had given her the gold trinity knot necklace for her sixteenth birthday, explaining that the ovals represented their nuclear family, and the center circle signified the love that held them together. She has worn it every day since her mother died. The trinity knot, her family's special symbol, is dear to her heart. She prays that her future family will reflect this tradition.

CHAPTER 13

The King Ranch

Gabby unlocks the front door, inhaling the deep scent of the place she prefers to call home. Matthew fell asleep during the drive, so she carefully sets the car seat in the safety of the living room lounge chair.

After opening the drapes, allowing light to flood through the sliding glass door, she turns toward the small sidebar in the corner of the living room and pours a healthy portion of Garrison Brothers Cowboy bourbon. It's midday, but she doesn't care. She swirls the dark amber liquid in the glass and offers a toast to her dead husband. This bourbon is the "drink of choice" for the men in the family. She creeps past her sleeping baby, then retreats to a rocking chair on the front porch.

She takes a deep breath to help settle her spirit in the present, allowing her to enjoy the details of the moment. Her breathing finds the perfect rhythm to match the moans of the wooden planks beneath her chair as she rocks. She lifts her glass, noting the smell of pine, followed by a smokiness, then finally tastes hints of cherry before the numbing potion travels to warm her stomach.

Her eyes detect a clue to the arrival of fall in the hint of yellow on the trees. Her ears heed the frogs' croaking and the distant bellow of a calf. She looks at the wispy clouds and offers gratitude and praise for this slice of heaven.

The vibrating phone in her pocket threatens her peacefulness. Richard's name flashes across the screen. Still miffed with how things were left between them this morning, she ignores the call. He can leave a message. This special time is *her* time, and no one will steal it.

During the few weeks since Richard pulled her up on the stage at an election debate, their relationship has taken a one-eighty turn. But has it? Hasn't their relationship always been a rollercoaster of emotions? It's unfair to blame the pressure of the election on their unsettling personal interactions.

She recalls family celebrations, and it's apparent that her father played a major role in those fond memories. Yet, she struggles to find similar enjoyable moments in her relationship with Richard. Many evenings their plans are thwarted because of a work crisis or frequent phone calls. Other than stealing a few moments for a romp in bed, they don't have much in common. When they first met, their relationship was different—they played tennis, laughed, went to clubs, and danced. Could it ever be like that again, or will this heavy political aura that suffocates their relationship remain?

She remembers their first go around five years ago. Even back then, their relationship revolved around his schedule and his wishes. She was never the center of his world. Is she selfish to want more? What will their relationship be like if he wins the election? She imagines time traveling for a heart-to-heart conversation with Jackie Kennedy. Jackie shared John with all of America. Gabby is only being asked to share Richard with Texas. Can she share someone who was never hers?

She had poured her whole being into their relationship the first time around. As time went on, he was unfaithful, and she was hurt. But when Brett came into her life, he made her believe again. He showed her the meaning of true love and the ability to care for someone with shared mutual respect. She fears that kind of love is a once-in-a-lifetime, never to come her way again. With Brett gone, she knows she doesn't love Richard as deeply, but she has never stepped away to question if he loves her. Is there truth to Amanda's words?

Her thoughts are interrupted by Ryder, Stan's dog, running down the lane toward her house. He bounds up the stairs and places his head on her lap.

"Hey, boy, where did you come from?" She pets the dog and nuzzles his soft neck. "You, my friend, are lucky. You have this carefree life…running over the meadows and the fields. Does your daddy know where you are?" From experience, she's aware that if Ryder is here, Stan is close by. He must have seen her car in the driveway, knowing that if he let Ryder roam, the dog would find his way to her house.

"How about a treat?" She returns with a large piece of jerky. Ryder eagerly accepts the treat and sits at her feet, gnawing away. "I was saving this for a special occasion. Yep, today, we're celebrating." She takes another swig of the bourbon and feels the alcohol tingle to her toes.

Her desire to reach an inner calmness is challenged by her chirping phone, so she pulls it from her pocket and listens to Richard's voicemail.

"You packed the wrong sneakers. These have the opposing team's colors. Bring another pair, and I'll stop by headquarters before the tennis match. Okay…umm…thanks."

Oh my—not happening. This morning she decided to pack and drive to the ranch without consulting Richard or her daddy. The political schedule of events shortened her last trip, and a repeat of that isn't in her future. He'll be mad that she's at the ranch.

Instead of a text, she dials his number. Richard never picks up his phone during the day, so she'll be responsible and leave a message. At least she won't be chastised for not returning his call. Let someone else do his bidding. Isn't that Amanda's job?

Movement on the gravel road by the creek gets her attention. The man's familiar limp tells her it's Stan, Rita's eldest son.

She waves, then yells, "Ryder's here!"

He waves back but doesn't answer until he gets to the end of her drive. "This is a surprise. What brings you here?"

"This is my home. I needed to get away…gain perspective." She takes another sip.

He motions toward her glass. "Starting early."

"It's been that kind of a day." She rubs her forehead. "Why are you home? The horse center doesn't close until 4:00 p.m."

"Guess you're not the only one who needs a new perspective." He looks at Ryder, happily chewing on the treat. "Are you spoiling my dog? No wonder he runs here whenever I open the door."

Ryder looks up but continues to eat the jerky.

"I'm drinking The Cowboy. Care to join? We can commiserate." She points to the adjacent rocking chair. "It's been a long time since we had a powwow on the porch."

"Don't mind if I do. I know where the booze is. You stay, and I'll get it."

When the thirty-seven-year-old dark-haired man returns with the bourbon bottle and a glass, she wonders if the anticipated second drink is for her problems or his own.

He pulls his rocking chair close to hers and clinks her glass. "Welcome home. I've missed you. I saw Matthew sleeping in his carrier; he's getting big."

"Good, I need a break."

Stan pushes a number into his phone. "Jamie, did you see who's here? Look out your window...I'm with her right now. Yes, he's sleeping. We'll bring him over when he wakes up. Dinner...set an extra plate; make that two if your invite extends to me. Marie? No, she's got some girl thing tonight."

"She's very excited. Hung up quick—something about making your favorite dessert. Would that be cherry pie, I suppose?"

"Absolutely. You remembered?"

"Of course. A mind like an elephant. Saw your picture in the paper...with Richard...

again. It's almost a daily thing. What was it like with the governor and his wife?"

"It was okay."

"Just okay? It could be your future residence." He sits forward in his chair. "Your dream deserves a little more excitement."

"It's complicated." She gulps her drink.

"Tell me—what's going on?"

She drains her glass.

"Geez, take it easy. This stuff is pure alcohol. Tell me. I'm not leaving until you do." He holds her hand. The gesture is kind—a rare thing these days. A lump forms in her throat. He squeezes her hand.

She turns away before answering. "It's Richard."

Stan throws his hands up in the air. "As always. What did he do now?" He reaches for the bottle and pours another into his glass.

"Why do you say it with that tone?" She leans back in her chair, anticipating his negative response.

"Gabby, Richard is Richard. A zebra doesn't change his stripes. You're a silly girl if you expect different."

"I thought he'd changed."

"And why would he change? People are motivated to change. First, it's looking like he'll win the election. Second, he has King paving the way like he's freakin' royalty. Third, he's got you." Stan's voice trails off, and his eyes drop. "Seems pretty much perfect. Like I said, he isn't motivated to be anything but the way he is."

She runs her fingers through her hair. "But it's not perfect."

"Not for you. From what I see, you need to decide how much of *you*, you're willing to sacrifice." He shakes his head.

She bites her nail.

"What do you want? It's that simple. I can't tell you what to do, but I will share what I see. Richard is out for himself." He drains his glass. "I've said enough. Think about it, Gabby. You're always putting everyone else first. Don't make your decision for Richard. Don't make your decision for your dad. Make the right decision for you and Matthew."

He stands, holding the bottle. "Come on, Ryder. Let's go." He turns to face her, and she notes sadness in him. "Think about it. He leans down to kiss her on the forehead. "I'm glad you're here." He motions toward the bourbon bottle. "I'm taking this with me. Take

82

care of your son. And I'll see you at dinner. Call me if you want to walk over together."

Disappointed that he is leaving, she watches him walk down the lane with Ryder at his side. He has an uncanny way of always showing up, and she notes how his quick wit gave a voice to her dilemma without an explanation. Then, he followed through with an answer. *Do what is right for me?* It's as though he suspected her situation. Apparently, her private relationship is transparent; first, the confrontation with Amanda and now a second time with Stan's conversation.

The warmth of the alcohol flows through her veins, and a soft dullness like a blanket covers her brain, but she recalls his words: "I've said enough." If he continued, what more would he have offered? When he first approached, she believed that they would be on the porch solving the world's problems and laughing so hard until they cried, or at least reminiscing until Matthew finished his nap. However, he left abruptly, leaving her standing in a shadow of loneliness. She reaches for her trinity knot necklace and slides the knot back and forth in rhythm with her rocking chair. Was he upset with her, or is something else bothering him? They never got around to discussing his problem. She regrets not asking.

A few hours later, during dinner at the main house with Rusty and Jamie, Gabby is laughing until the tears roll down her face. Stan is known for captivating his audience with his tales. Tonight is no exception with his lively storytelling. He must have made peace with whatever was on his mind earlier. Jamie bounces Matthew on her lap, and Rusty is feeding Ryder bites of meat under the table. The fried chicken and dumplings are the best she's eaten in a long time. Nothing like good Southern fare, and the company is priceless. She can let her hair down. This is the closest she's come to being herself in months.

On the campaign trail, she has to be on guard. It's exhausting to think through every word and action, to be careful so the media doesn't misconstrue what she says. It's a circus, and she's a performer. However, instead of the once-happy showgirl in a beautiful sequined outfit, she's turned into a clown with a sad painted face.

She's surprised at how content she is here at the ranch because that wasn't always the case. This past summer marked the one-year anniversary of Brett's death. For survival, she ran from their home. Surrounded by the painful reminders of her once blissful life with the man who made her whole was too much to bear. Working through her grief initially with a psychologist and now adding both distance and time, she's better equipped to put things in proper perspective.

Back then, it was hard to believe that her life would continue with him gone. Why did she think that escaping her roots would provide comfort? At first, life in the city provided a distraction. Now, it's more of a nuisance. The ranch has always been her life; she was foolish to think otherwise.

She did leave once before. She traveled to New York City after she graduated with her art degree. Her dream to wow the critics in the SOHO district with her unusual perspectives and brilliant colors was slashed. She was never able to publish her art in prestigious journals and couldn't sell enough to cover her rent. After two years, she gave up on her dream and returned to her family, content to exhibit her work at Rita's gallery.

If Richard wins the election, she'll be expected to reside in the city to stand by his side. Most people living a demanding, public life find a way to divide their time between their job during the week and a weekend escape to reboot. For some, that means the mountains; for others, their retreat is near the sea. For her, home is the ranch. But Richard thrives only in the city. Can there be a healthy mix of residences to keep them both happy? Once again, Stan's words surface. *How much of yourself are you willing to sacrifice?*

"Gabby, what was that guy's name, the guy from the interview?" Stan scratches his neck before reaching for another piece of cherry pie. "You still with us? You look as though you are a million miles away."

"Sorry, I was thinking."

"Care to share?"

"No, it's nothing." His stare makes her chew the inside of her cheek. "Really, it's nothing. I'm tired. It's been a long day." She stretches. Stan breaks his gaze.

He slaps his knees. "Yes, I agree. I've had a rough day, too." He stands. "Jamie, Rusty, thanks for your kind hospitality. Another fabulous dinner. I'll see Gabby and the little man home."

"Stan, stay, please, don't leave on my account." Their eyes meet, and she detects a mix of sadness. Or is it concern? Perhaps both. *Why was his day rough?*

With the lights of the main house behind them, Stan and Gabby walk down the lane that leads to their houses. She carries Tupperware of left-over cherry pie, and he carries Matthew with Ryder by his side.

Getting close to their prospective houses, she asks, "What stars are out tonight?"

"Can't see many. It's a waxing moon, and there are clouds. It's not the best night, but I'm sure you can find one star to wish upon. Do you still make that a habit?"

He stops walking and shifts Matthew in his arms. The moonlight touches his face, and its shine contrasts with the hollows in shadow.

"Not in the city. It's hard to see the stars with the ambient light. Being here reminds me how much my soul feeds on this." She points to the vast surroundings that know no limits.

"Feeds on what, exactly?" He lowers his face and snuggles with her son.

"You know, all of this."

"Spell it out. You need to give it a voice. Speaking will make your inner thoughts real. Remember, I've been in therapy."

She pinches her lips together and takes a deep breath. "I'm suffocating in the city. I'm concerned about what the future holds if Richard wins the election."

"Okay, that's a start. Continue."

"I'm concerned that I'll live in that historic mansion with my life strewn all over the front page of *The Statesman*. No matter what I do, someone will criticize me. I got a taste of that already, and it's nasty."

"That's a politician's life. It will be your life. You're making a choice." He looks up at the sky as if he's searching for his wishing star.

"Gabby, you never answered the first question."

"What is that?"

"What does your soul need? What feeds your soul?"

She pauses, gathering her thoughts. "Nature, the open space, the sky filled with stars. Freedom." She gives a small chuckle. "Yes, freedom, how ironic. I scrawled the word *freedom* on the painting I created one sleepless night after Richard announced his candidacy. That message sprang from my heart. It was meant for me—before

Richard adopted it for his campaign slogan. Now I'm surrounded by it every time I walk down the street. It's on the storefronts; it's on the campaign buttons. I created this freedom platform, and ironically it's becoming my prison."

"And what does your future hold if Richard doesn't become our next governor? Will he ever permanently live here at the ranch?"

"Never. Richard is not a rancher. You've seen him on a horse." She laughs. "He'll go back to his practice. Run again for another term in the Senate." She rubs her forehead. "But he'll win. Daddy will make that happen even if it takes his last living breath."

"So, either way, the ranch isn't Richard's future. Are you okay with that? It's the opposite of nature and open spaces."

"I thought I was, but now, after experiencing public life, I'm not so sure." She smiles, looking at the man who seems to speak from wisdom, carrying her sleeping son. "You, Stan, are a good therapist."

"It's good that I got something for my money. Giving voice is the first step to understanding your inner turmoil. Now comes the second part—action."

His intense stare burns her soul. She turns and resumes walking.

They arrive at her porch. After unlocking the door, he follows her inside and lays Matthew in his crib. "Sleep well, little man."

She notes a gentleness. He'll make a good father someday.

"Stan, what's going on? I'm sorry I didn't ask earlier. You said that you had a rough day. Your turn to give a voice."

His smile is genuine. "Our talk tonight is helping. Listening to you speaks to my soul. Thank you." He pulls her in for a hug and kisses her on the forehead. "See you tomorrow.

I know the way out." He turns and leaves.

She smiles, content to watch the peaceful face of her son. *Stan has spent more time with Matthew in the past few hours than Richard has in a week.* Stan had avoided answering her question. What could be bothering him?

CHAPTER 14

Stan is known to drop everything and do anything for Gabby. In return, she reciprocates by anticipating his needs and helping whenever possible. A good example is when Stan needed rehab after a motorcycle accident two years ago. Gabby had wiggled one million bucks out of her daddy to expand the near-bankrupt Veterans Horse Center, enabling it to treat not only veterans but also other patients. This allowed Stan to do physical therapy at the center, just thirty minutes from the ranch, rather than driving back to the city.

During that time, Stan had taken to country living and created a life here with a new job and, later, a house on the ranch, just a short jaunt down the road from her own.

Since opening the center, Stan and Gabby have divided their business duties. Besides helping with the cattle at busy times on the ranch, Stan is the workhorse of the center. He keeps it running smoothly by supervising the veterans who care for the stables and the horses, hiring staff needed for the equine and hippotherapy, and keeping the books.

But lately, many of Gabby's administrative duties have also fallen on Stan's shoulders now that she and Richard are engaged.

A year ago, they hired Marie as the equine therapy psychologist. Marie had previously been a victim of human trafficking. Luckily, Stan had found her near death on the outskirts of the King Ranch and saved her life. After her recovery, which included the use of equine therapy, she was so impressed that she got training for her own certification. She applied for the job at the center, was hired, and within a short period of time, she and Stan became a couple.

Gabby's involvement with horse therapy originated in a different way. She gives all the credit to Stan for introducing her to equine therapy. A year before his motorcycle accident, he had taken Gabby to a horse farm in Virginia owned and operated by his friend, Andrew Green, and his partner, Eric Lang. The couple has years of experience in equine therapy, and after learning of Gabby's idea to expand a center in Texas to help their friend with his rehab, they enthusiastically offered their expertise. Over the past year, the new and improved equine center has gained respect from positive patient reviews, encouraging more doctors to use their services. The business grew, making it possible to help more people than originally projected.

Today at the equine center, Marie leans her small frame on the office door, watching the man who made an attempt four months ago to cement their relationship into something permanent. He had gotten down on one knee and proposed, but she has yet to say yes. She removes her cowboy hat and runs her fingers through her dark brown tresses. "I just said good-bye to the last patient of the day."

"Good, let me finish filing these folders, then I'll help get the rest of this place back in order." Stan turns from the metal cabinet to face her. "While the cleaning folks are here, I can drive the truck to the nursery and load the plants Gab ordered for the dedication party. You want to come along?"

She scratches her head. "I have so much to do before tomorrow night. I should get my nails done. This job is hard on my hands, not to mention the number it does on my feet trapped in these boots day after day."

His eyes lower. "You sure? We haven't spent much time together, and tomorrow is going to be crazy. It would be nice to have an evening to ourselves."

"I'm sorry, big guy, but this girl has got to look her best."

His face still turns red when she uses that pet name. He pulls her in for a hug.

"If you're not going to the nursery with the big guy, you can…" He kisses her long and hard before whispering in her ear words that make her giggle.

"Stan, we can't."

He kisses her again, then pulls her shirt out of her jeans.

"Excuse me," Gregg, the veteran with a prosthetic leg, says with a chuckle. "Oh, to be young." He clicks his tongue on the roof of his mouth.

A red-faced Marie backs away from Stan and looks out the window, tucking her shirt into her jeans.

"Misty, the gray mare, is favoring her left back foot. Thought you should know." He exits as quickly and silently as he entered.

Marie slaps Stan on the arm.

He laughs and then dodges at her. She positions herself on the opposite side of the desk.

"I can play this game." He leaps over the desk.

She backs up. "Stan, be serious."

"I am. Come on, go with me." He pouts, rubbing his leg.

"Tomorrow is a really big day. We're dedicating the center. With Richard here, the press will follow, and Gabby always looks perfect. Then there's Amanda. You want me to look good, right?"

"Women, why do you compare yourselves to each other? You're fine just the way you are. Who are you looking good for? And if you're getting your nails done, you can show them off by wearing my ring."

"Stan, don't start with that again. Not now."

"If not now, when Marie?"

"You're pressuring me."

"I haven't brought up the subject in over three months."

"So why today?"

"With the dedication of this center where we both spend our days, it would be nice if the woman I share my nights with would dedicate her life to our relationship. Isn't that reason enough?" He searches her face for an answer. "I'm nearly forty, and it's ridiculous to introduce you as my girlfriend. That's something a teenager boasts about."

She bites her lip. "I can't discuss this now. My nail appointment is in thirty minutes. Raincheck, please?"

"Whatever…you best be on your way." He waves his arm to shoo her out of the office.

CHAPTER 15

E arly the following afternoon, Gabby stands in the parking lot, shielding her eyes from the sun's glare to view the newly installed sign attached to the metal roof: The Matthews Horse Therapy Center. Her heart leaps at the thought of honoring Brett; he would be proud. Seeing a physical validation of her hard work makes her composure short-lived as the tears drop from her chin. Her emotions spring from the joy of creating a legacy for Brett's life mixed with sadness that still presides over his absence.

The sign's emerald-green background symbolizes the color of Brett's eyes, while the bold white letters add a nice contrast. The sign is the finishing touch to the newly renovated center, with services in addition to equine therapy for behavioral issues, substance abuse, depression, and anxiety, including hippotherapy, which uses the horse's movements to engage the motor and sensory systems of the client.

The center, located deep in the country, will transform lives as it allows rural clients to get their therapy without traveling the long drive to and from the city. Helping others is her mission, and she feels empowered by the legacy she's creating to honor her husband's life.

Now is the better time to experience the gamut of her emotions because this evening will require her to be composed as she stands on stage for the grand opening. Unlike trailing Richard on his mission to be elected, she's taking the lead to honor Brett.

Gazing at the sign one more time and nodding in satisfaction at the craftsmanship, she pulls her shoulders back and climbs the steps. There's plenty of work to be completed in the next few hours before the guests arrive.

Since yesterday, the reception area has been transformed into a garden with plants in the center, filling the entire space. There are ferns among them, but it's the sweet fragrant gardenias that bring fond memories.

"Stan, thanks for getting the plants."

She walks down the hall to his office, unsure that he heard her remarks of gratitude. He's hunched over the ledger.

"Thanks for picking up the plants." She plops into the chair.

He taps the pen on his desk. "You're welcome. I didn't know where you wanted them."

"They're fine where they are. The event planner will be here in a few minutes with her whole team, and she'll place them. After to-night, I thought we could plant the gardenias in the front beds."

He wrinkles his brow. "There aren't any flower beds."

"Precisely. We're going to put some in."

His eyes sparkle. "That's not in my job description."

"You don't have a job description. But I can make one." She twirls a strand of her blond hair. "The sign looks great. Now that the reno-vations are complete, the next chore is the flower beds."

"The sign gives the center a professional look. It's good."

She turns around in her chair. "Where's Marie?"

"At home, getting pretty. She feels inferior to you and Amanda, so she's doing all that girly stuff…hair…waxing…I can't keep track of it. Why aren't you doing all that stuff?"

She looks down at her nails. "These will have to do. I want everything to be perfect, and time is running out. I brought my clothes with me. I'll change here."

"Isn't that why you hired an event planner to take care of all these last-minute details?"

"Call it a trust issue. The only way to achieve perfection is to make it a DIY project, do it yourself."

"A large, heavy box came for you late yesterday." With eyes down on his ledger, he motions to the large narrow box out by the hallway near the kitchenette.

"It came yesterday, and you didn't tell me!" She leaps up from the chair. "I can't wait to see it. Can you help me?"

"Sure, it's a painting, right? It says *framing* on the invoice I had to sign."

"It's my surprise. See that empty wall?" She points to the wall in the main room. "Wait until you see this. I hope it gives the impact I want."

She rushes to grab scissors from the drawer and dashes toward the box. She's careful as she cuts through the tape and lifts the staples with scissors.

"Here, let me do that. My knife will be better for the job." Stan moves her to the side. "We can't have you cutting yourself."

"The framer told me he was coming to hang it this afternoon. This will make tonight's dedication perfect." She struggles with the box. "You take this side, and I'll take the other."

Working in tandem, they pull the five-by-seven-foot framed painting out of the box and protected wooden crate. Next, Gabby removes the plastic packing to reveal a painting of the Texas landscape with a cowboy leading a horse into the sunset. Gabby places her hand over her heart. The dark wooden frame provides a sharp contrast to the mellow colors of the landscape melting into the fading sun.

As the sign made the horse center look professional, the frame does the same for her painting. In the silence, her heart pounds. Even though the cowboy's back is to the viewer, there's no doubt for anyone who knew him that it is Brett.

"You painted this?" Stan scratches his chin. "I've never seen you paint anything but abstracts and knots."

In a low, weak voice, she says, "Let's just say I was motivated by the subject matter."

He steps away for a better perspective. "It's wonderful…incredible, actually."

But the art doesn't depict the rivers she cried during its creation. She lowers her eyes and turns away, determined not to give in to the waterworks. However, the tears refuse to obey, and she sucks in a deep breath, batting them away.

"Hey, hey." He reaches for her and brings her in close, stroking her hair. The moisture soaking through his shirt begs him to share in her grief. "Talk to me."

"Brett has reached that distant horizon and left me stranded. Abandoned. Sometimes it feels like he left me just yesterday. Other times it seems like I have been living this dreadful existence for decades." She sniffles. "I have memories of a thousand beautiful sunsets, but since his accident, the sunsets have been clouded in pain." Her body trembles. "I thought I was better."

He turns her to face the painting. "You are better. It takes time. Your sunsets will be beautiful again. This painting is a great tribute. I see the sun rays glimmering across the prairie as a sign of hope. You painted hope, not despair."

She leans into his shoulder for support and studies the sun's ascending rays, dipping below the horizon. Maybe Stan's positive interpretation is valid.

"You always know the right thing to say." She pinches her lips together. "Tonight marks a milestone. Hanging this painting and dedicating this center gives Brett a proper legacy."

Stan's strong arms keep her from collapsing. Once again, he is an anchor, providing security in her sea of uncertainty.

"Yes, you'll have some closure." He pulls her arm. "I know what you need. Come with me."

He leads her out the back door toward the stable. In the forward stall is Misty, the gray mare.

"Hey, girl." Gabby strokes the mare's face. "What's wrong with her leg?" She points to the cooling boot on the horse's back leg.

"An infection of some sort…antibiotics and the cold boot to reduce the swelling. She'll be fine in a few days." He pats her side. "She's a bit lonely. We took her off the schedule to give that leg a rest. Poor thing, she thinks she's being punished."

Gabby lays her head on the mare's warm neck. The horse turns her head, welcoming this act of compassion and companionship. Aware of the mare's breathing, her own breaths slow to match the rhythm. The quiet and the smell of the hay exude calmness, and the rubber-band tension between her shoulder blades releases. With her eyes closed, she twirls the strands of Misty's black mane through her fingers. The mare's neck hugs her in response. This nonverbal communication is precious.

Gabby's ringing phone breaks the silence.

"The frame guy is here to hang the painting."

Stan smiles and wipes bits of black mascara from under her eyes. "There, you're more like yourself again. A little equine therapy works wonders." He chuckles.

"I needed that. Thanks."

"Misty needed that, too. You should spend more time together." He nods and pats the mare's side. "But first, let's get your painting hung. It's perfect for the center. Makes me wonder how many other talents you're hiding." He winks and grabs her hand. "Let's not keep him waiting."

The door to the horse center opens as they cross the corral, still holding hands. Marie's stare cuts like a sword. With guilt and shame rising in her chest, Gabby drops Stan's hand.

"Marie, when did you get here?" Stan squints in the sun.

"Just now. I let the frame guy in, but I didn't know where you wanted the painting hung."

Stan attempts to plant a kiss, but Marie turns her face.

"I'm surprised you're here. I thought your appointments would take all day."

"No, finished by noon. I decided to help set up."

"Your hair looks great." Stan reaches for her long brown tresses.

Gabby flashes a smile. "Marie, thanks, that's really kind." She pats her on the shoulder, then takes her hand. "Come, I need your opinion. How high on the wall should we hang this painting?" She pulls Marie with her into the center. "He's right; your hair does look great.

Who's your stylist?" Before Marie has a chance to respond, Gabby stops and turns. "Stan, you coming?"

"I'll be along in a bit. I forgot something in the stable." He tips his hat at the two women.

CHAPTER 16

The equine horse center buzzes with the hum of conversation. It's early in the evening, and Gabby takes inventory of her guests. As usual, King and Rita are surrounded by his circle of prominent business associates. King stands close to Rita, holding on to her arm. The sight of her daddy, who found a second chance for love, makes her heart leap.

The line for the bartender is growing, and waiters carry full trays of appetizers. Should she have hired additional staff? At present, it seems that drinking is more of a priority than eating. It's a blessing the weather is cooperating, as the fall evening temps allow for mingling outdoors, inviting guests to the porch to enjoy the soft notes of the small band, Avenue. The group was a great recommendation from Marie since her love of music makes her an expert on local talent.

On several occasions, Gabby has heard raised voices between Stan and Marie over her interest in the nightlife as it seems to magnify their thirteen-year age gap. After work, Marie wants to hit the bar scene, and Stan prefers to spend time at the ranch. Every relationship has its challenges.

She checks her watch. Richard should have been here by now. She'll have to delay her presentation for the dedication. Doesn't he understand the importance of this evening?

Kristine Walker approaches. "Thank you, Ms. King, for giving me exclusive coverage for tonight's events. My boss was impressed. I have Gus, my cameraman, waiting along the side of the building so as not to disturb your guests. We can bypass using larger lights on tripods because the natural light is sufficient. They draw attention, and I understand that you wish us to be as unintrusive as possible."

Before Gabby can respond, a black limo crawls up the drive, interrupting their conversation. The driver hops out and then opens the back door. Richard emerges with Amanda on his heels. He holds out his arm to assist the brunette. Did she stumble because of her five-inch heels, or is she inebriated? God, Gabby hopes it's the former.

Even though this event honors Brett's life and draws attention to the horse center, as Richard's campaign manager, Amanda knows his attendance demonstrates his compassion for those struggling. It's good press. Foremost, the dedication of the horse center to Brett should be tonight's topic of conversation, not Richard Wright, and certainly not distraction caused by poor judgment from his drunken campaign manager.

Kristine Walker brushes past Gabby, rushing to get to Richard. This was not their agreement. Didn't they just have this conversation? Already, his arrival is creating a commotion. Heat rises in her chest. She wills it to dissipate, determined to stay calm and controlled. The camera crew runs to Walker's side, and the beam from the camera signals they are live.

"Mr. Wright, a few words for our viewers." Kristine smiles and bats her eyes.

"Of course, anything for a beautiful woman and for the great citizens of Texas." He steps back to keep the bright camera lights out of his eyes. Amanda remains by his side, her arm looped through his. "I'm very sensitive to the needs of those who require therapy, and this center will serve hundreds of patients. When I'm elected, money will be budgeted annually for treatment centers like this all over the state that help others heal."

"You seem passionate about helping those in need."

"I was taught to put others first. You'll see changes in this direction with me at the helm." He flashes a wide grin and points at the camera. "Remember to vote and make the right choice."

Still hanging on his arm, Amanda takes an unsteady half-step forward. "Wright for Governor is the right choice." She swings their arms up together.

Gabby's stomach churns. She lowers her head, avoiding eye contact with guests, and makes her way back to the building. Once on the porch, she pulls the clapper on the cast iron bell mounted by the front door. The loud ring breaks the guests' attention on Richard's interview and stops the music.

"Time for the dedication." She lifts a glass of champagne taken from the waiter's tray, then encourages her guests to gather inside, offering each a token of a smile, a kind word, or a gentle touch. She nods to Stan and Marie to join her in the great room in front of her painting.

To get everyone's attention, Stan clicks his champagne glass with a spoon, but the loud hum of conversation continues, so he places two fingers in his mouth and whistles. The loud screech does the trick, and all eyes face the trio.

Gabby reaches for Stan's hand to steady herself, and his eyes reassure her that she can do this. The fire in her gut from Richard's entrance sparks a determination to stand firm with confidence and give Brett his rightful tribute. This night is about her late husband and the horse center. *Richard Wright, you should be here by my side. You should be supporting me and my efforts. No surprise that you're not.*

She scans the gathering crowd. Front and center, her daddy stands with his arm around Rita. His seed money enabled the institution to grow into what it's known for today. He's a good man, and she's forever grateful for his trust and support of her vision.

Finally, Richard passes with purpose through the crowd, urgent to join them. She takes a deep breath and starts speaking before he can claim his place beside her. Her voice trembles with shaky first words, but warmth radiates from her heart and travels upward, causing her face to glow and giving her confidence. Her voice increases in strength and passion.

"Welcome, all, and thank you for spending your evening with us." A hush prevails over the room. "First, I would like to thank Wayne King, my generous and supportive daddy. His confidence that the team of Stan Adams, Marie Gonzales, and myself could make this institution one of the best horse therapy centers in Texas was key to our success." She turns to acknowledge Stan and Marie, then joins her guests in clapping to honor King. Then, with a conviction for her meaningful task, her voice grows stronger.

"Tonight, I have the honor of dedicating this worthy institution to Brett Matthews. Brett was a loyal and enthusiastic horseman and the love of my life." She turns to give attention to the painting hanging behind her. "I titled this painting of a cowboy leading his horse into the sunset "Final Horizon," and next to it, I have placed the National Professional Rodeo plaque given earlier this year as a memorial for Brett for his accomplishments and devotion to the sport of rodeo. Rightly so, these items belong here in the newly expanded and renovated horse center. Now, please raise your glasses as we dedicate this building to Brett Matthews, my late husband, and rename the center, The Matthews Horse Therapy Center." The clicking of glasses and the outburst of cheers ring throughout as balloons fall from a net attached to the ceiling. On cue, the band strikes up a lively tune.

Did anyone notice how her voice quivered on those last words? Water fills her eyes, and she bites her lip. She says a prayer before she takes a sip of champagne. Effervescent bubbles kiss her nose, reminding her of the many times she and Brett shared a toast. *This one's for you, my love.* A lopsided smile graces her face.

She becomes aware that someone is near, and Stan whispers in her ear, "You did awesome." Then he brushes her cheek with a light kiss. She leans into his body for support and closes her eyes. She feels safe.

The moment is cut short as Marie praises and hugs her, the first in a line of many guests. Kristine Walker's team snaps a few shots.

"I need one with Senator Wright," Kristine Walker says in a commanding tone.

"Where is Richard?" Gabby says, searching for her fiancé.

A minute later, Marie comes forward, dragging Richard on her arm. Gabby feels his cold stare. No words are exchanged between them.

The line to congratulate her thins after an hour, and she finally gets a moment with her daddy.

"I've waited all evening for a dance. Shall we?" He holds out his hand. Smiling, he takes his daughter in his arms, eyes shining. "I'm a very proud father. Brett would be proud, too, princess. You articulated your message in a matter worthy of any great spokesperson. Richard had best be careful." He clears his throat. "Perhaps you should be running for governor." He kisses her hand and pulls her in tighter to his large frame. She buries her face in his shoulder. Their body language trumps any conversation, and they dance. All who watch witness the overwhelming love between father and daughter.

Their intimate moment is interrupted by a tap on King's shoulder. Brandon Matthews stands near with bold confidence.

He extends his hand. "May I have the honor of a dance with the beautiful hostess?"

King focuses on his daughter, searching for a clue. Brandon Mathews wasn't on her guest list, and how did she miss his arrival? Is this another one of his surprises? Nodding to her daddy and signaling to grant Brandon's request, King bestows a kiss on her forehead, then bows before backing away. Quickly, she's in the arms of the tall F1 team engineer.

Brandon smiles. "You seem surprised to see me."

Although she does her best to avoid eye contact, her fingertips gently embrace his muscular frame beneath the thin fabric of his shirt, and once again, her heart stirs at the similarities he shares with her late husband. "I didn't know that you were here. I combed through the RSVPs a few hours ago, and no, I don't recall your name on that list."

"Steve Prime extended an invite. I hope it's not a problem." He clears his throat, and she pulls back to catch a glimpse of his grin. "As a major donor to Senator Wright's campaign and our racing team, I thought it best not to dismiss his invitation. Attending a dedication to my brother's memorial seems like the right family thing to do."

As she is concentrating on his words, she steps on his shoe. "So sorry." The heat rises in her face.

"You would appreciate that I jumped through hoops to make tonight happen. Originally, I was to work with the team, reviewing the results from the simulator, but when I want something, I try my best to make it happen." He winks.

She tenses as he speaks. He smells of pine, like when they met at the Foundation Room. This time, he pulls away. She lifts her gaze, and his brown eyes fix on her face with a seemingly mischievous sparkle. That, combined with the upward curve of his mouth, makes the resemblance to Brett striking. Her heart quickens.

"I'll leave if you want. I mean you no harm or discomfort. I want to get acquainted with my family."

He seems sincere. She turns, hoping to disguise her anxiety. His surprise tactics, which give him the upper hand, always put her on edge. With a stronger voice, she says, "This night is about Brett. Family should be here. But it's still very awkward."

"I understand that it will take time." The compassion in his tone is unexpected yet calming.

She feels the tension leave his shoulders, and he hums with the music. The sound is another innocent likeness to his twin since Brett did the same thing. There is no way Brandon Matthews could obtain that tidbit of knowledge from the internet. He is probably clueless that his gestures link him to his brother. If she let her defenses slide, she could close her eyes, and it would be as if Brett had returned. The thought is enticing as well as disturbing.

"Your painting is exquisite. Is it for sale?"

"Thank you for the compliment. Its resting place is here at the center."

"You could paint one of me standing next to a race car." He stops dancing and holds her away as though searching for an answer. "I would love to visit the gallery and see more of your art."

"Perhaps," she says, laying her head back on his shoulder. "Perhaps."

When the music stops, he releases his grip and bows. "Goodnight, Miss King. It has been a pleasure, as always." With a turn, he is gone.

Supervising the clean-up crew, Gabby takes off her shoes and rests her feet on one of the chair arms. Stan plops down next to her, carrying a bottle of bourbon and two glasses.

"Where's Marie?"

"She went with Richard, your dad, Rita, that car fellow, and several of those big corporate guys down to that small local bar on the corner, the one near the main road."

"Was Amanda with them?"

"Yes. Marie thought she should go and keep an eye on her. But I think that's just an excuse. Marie likes all the attention that comes from hanging with Richard. I hope they all behave because someone will be certain to post on social media—*the gubernatorial candidate visits local bar.* Let the gossip roll." He pours the bourbon into the glasses. "I can't even imagine the hashtags."

"So…why are you here? You should go too. Be with them. It doesn't take both of us to lock the doors."

He hands her a glass of bourbon. "The bar scene is not my thing—especially not with that crowd. I'd rather be here." He clinks her glass with his own. "You did great tonight. Nice party…good speech." He lifts his glass, then clinks hers a second time. "To Brett," he says and takes a sip.

"To Brett." The amber liquid warms her throat. "This dedication, along with hanging my painting and the plaque, has given me some closure. Don't judge me…it's weird, but I feel empowered." She swirls the ice in her glass. "Plus, I actually enjoyed talking with Brandon after I got over the shock of seeing him here."

"You two seemed pretty cozy…dancing." He raises his eyebrows.

She turns away, ignoring his remark. Yes, Brandon is an interesting addition to her life, but it's not a topic for discussion on the night of the center's dedication to Brett. She takes another sip of the bourbon and changes the subject. "Richard is pissed."

"I noticed he was a bit off."

"He barely spoke two words to me."

"I'm sorry. Makes sense, though; he wasn't the center of attention."

"I can't imagine what Amanda was thinking. Showing up tipsy, stumbling out of the limo. One gets the impression they were drinking the entire ride from town. Not the right public image for the senator. Perhaps they do make the perfect pair." She gives a faint hint of a grin, then turns to catch his reaction. When he meets her gaze, she says, "She loves him."

He shakes his head as if dismissing her remark. "You don't know that."

"I do know that…she told me."

Again, he raises his eyebrows.

"She ambushed me a few weeks ago…said they were great together and I should go back to the ranch where I belong." She avoids his expression by pretending to be interested in her sunset painting and biting the inside of her cheek. She says that Richard is with me only because of Daddy. They do seem happy, and they certainly spend enough time together. What do you see?"

He looks down at his boots. "I can't answer that."

"And why not?" She turns in her chair to face him. "You're smart. You've got eyes."

"Because I'm biased." He chuckles. "I'm the last person you should be asking." He gulps the bourbon, and she can tell by his grimace that it must have burned sliding down to his stomach.

"Stan, you're the only person I can trust." She touches his hand. "I value your opinion."

"Gab, you can trust yourself. Listen to your heart. You used the word *empowered*. What is your heart telling you?" His smile shines as if the answer should be obvious.

He wraps his fingers around her hand. "Come on, let me take you home. No sense both of us driving. Let's get these folks out of here. It's been a long day." His smile is reassuring, and she wonders why she can't talk to Richard as easily as she does with Stan.

They're quiet on the drive home, and the silence is eerie. Usually, their talk is spontaneous as they easily jump from one subject to another. Once arriving at her front door, he turns off the engine. Before she gathers her purse, he leaps out and opens the door. "Gabby, about our talk earlier…umm, you know how I feel about you…right?"

She lifts her eyes to his face shimmering in the moonlight. Time freezes, intensifying the sounds of the night—the croaking of frogs by the creek louder, the distant cry of a coyote closer. The creek babbles as if serenading the stars. She searches his face, surprised by his question and unsure how he expects her to answer. Is this a rhetorical question?

110

Her voice escapes. The seconds last an eternity; in that eternity, his eyes reveal a doorway to his soul, and she has been given passage.

"You know that I love you." His touch on her arm tightens.

His admission is clear. There is no misunderstanding. She furrows her brow, and her mouth drops. How should she respond? His eyes search her face for an answer. This invitation to expose her heart adds a new dimension to an existing conflict. It opens the wound that she's been nursing for weeks. The intensity unbearable, she turns away.

"Everyone knows. I've tried to move on. Lord knows I've tried." He leans in closer. "You asked me what I think." She doesn't turn her head. His lips gently touch hers, and she tastes the sweet bourbon that lingers. The kiss is gentle, warm, and soft like a virgin breeze, mysterious. She doesn't move. He's caught her off-guard, and a million notions race through her head. What does this mean? Is it the excitement of the night?

Gently, their lips meet again. This kiss is a bit more passionate but light nonetheless—a sort of tease. She responds to his invitation, desiring more. It's like a new dessert; at first, one might hesitate to try, but once the sweetness is known, one can't get enough. He pulls away, leaving her both astonished and denied.

Without another word, he turns and gets in his truck. She follows the taillights as they drive down the lane, fading into the night. His kisses have left her giddy and mystified. She closes her eyes and relives the moment, etching every detail into the vault in her brain. Of all nights, why tonight? They've known each other for years. She turns the engagement ring on her finger. It's so complicated…Richard, the election, her daddy, Brandon Matthews, and now, Stan.

She felt empowered earlier tonight, but now she's puzzled. She's always attributed her affection for Stan as a family connection, never anything romantic. After the kiss, though, her feelings have changed. Stan says everyone knows he's in love with her, but he's with Marie, and she's with Richard. Is Stan also living a lie? Pretending?

He's not her type. However, that simple kiss has stirred emotions that have been hidden since Brett passed. Stan has been with her through many difficult times. Four years ago, when she and Brett had a disagreement, she recalls Stan sitting in the dark, a beer in his hand. His words come to mind. "I saw the way you look at him. You don't look at me in that way." That was years ago, before Brett's accident, before their wedding, before she buried Jacob, her stillborn child. There is a long history between when he spoke those words and now.

With her eyes closed, Gabby's memory turns back the months, then the years. She recalls confrontations between Stan and Brett. She thought all that had been resolved since it appeared the two men had called a truce. Was that Stan stepping down like a gentleman, accepting Brett as her choice?

Since Stan spoke those words, he found Marie. During a summertime girl chat on the porch, Rita mentioned that Stan had bought an engagement ring and was waiting for Marie to accept. She's aware that the two have disagreements, but doesn't every couple? She thought he loved Marie. His words, "Everyone knows," and "I've always loved you," churn in her mind. How could she have been so blind?

However, since Brett died, everyone would agree that Stan has been her rock. She has leaned on him repeatedly. It was Stan who brought her a tree and decorations the first Christmas after Brett passed, a time when she wanted to stay in bed and let Father Christmas pass without stopping. She reached out to Stan and asked him to drive her to the hospital when she was in labor, and it was Stan who held her hand during Matthew's birth. Stan cleans her house gutters, reinforces the nails on her deck, and changes her light bulbs. Stan has always been there for her, has always come to her rescue, especially during Richard's absences.

Revisiting these critical moments that point to Stan's helpfulness, she bites her nails and concludes that Stan, being a good man, following in step with his character and reputation, would have never confessed his love while Brett was still alive. Her eyes open wide, and she brings her clenched fist to her heart. This new profound realization sends shock waves through her as she pictures Stan waiting patiently on the sidelines for the right day and hour.

While he waited, she made a critical mistake during one of the weakest moments of her life, a time when she wished to escape the pain, to be taken away from the brutal reality of caring for her comatose husband. Longing to feel warmth and love, Richard came to her door, and she welcomed his lovemaking. It was so simple. Perhaps some would call it reckless, but a few months later, that one decision probably saved her life because after Brett died, she was a mess, and the resulting pregnancy, that small life growing inside her, kept her from ending her life.

Now, she wonders if her future would have taken a different turn if Stan had knocked on her door that night instead of Richard.

How can Stan possibly love her? She is a terrible person and a horrible wife who slept with a former lover with her dying husband in the next room. Look at the mess she is making of her present life. The journey to the governor's mansion is not her dream; it's Richard's dream; it's her daddy's dream. And one leak of any of these past events to the press could jeopardize Richard's entire campaign. With less than two weeks before election day, her daddy could lose millions and would have thrown away this plan that's been five years in the making.

If the public knew the truth, Gabby would be judged unfit to be Texas's First Lady. For now, for her daddy's sake and for Richard, she must continue the charade and hope the ghosts of the past stay buried until Richard is announced governor. There is no other option.

She falls to her knees on the porch. Tears stream down her cheeks. She asks God for forgiveness for her past mistakes, for his guidance in future decisions, states her thankfulness for Stan's forgiveness, and asks her daddy to forgive her in advance for decisions that may not fit his grand plan. Will he understand if she decides to break her engagement to Richard?

A cool breeze blows, and she lifts her watery eyes to the stars. The dark-painted canvas displays millions of bright, twinkling bodies. She picks the one overhead, peering through the tree branches, and indulges her habit of wishing on a star. This wish differs from her past requests—for Brett to visit in her dreams. With the dedication over, she is motivated to close that chapter of her life and to continue moving forward, one little step at a time. She has asked the universe to guide her future steps.

Stan's house lights turn on down the lane, the yellow glow reflecting through the trees. Would it be reckless to knock on his door? If she had the courage to walk over there, would he invite her inside?

Tonight, you dedicated the newly renovated equine center. You were brave and committed to Brett's legacy. Tonight, Richard disappointed you. He showed up with Amanda and avoided you.

Could it be that he's jealous of your efforts to honor your dead husband?

Tonight, you danced with Brandon and had to stop yourself from imagining that he was Brett. Escaping into a relationship with Brandon would provide enough notes to fill a psychiatrist's notebook. Tonight, Stan kissed you, you didn't stop him, and then you kissed him back. What were you thinking?

Slow down, girlfriend. You're acting from a place of loneliness. Dancing with Brandon makes you feel like you are in your husband's arms. You miss the warmth. You miss having a man to love. It's been a long, stressful day, and you're too tired for big life-changing decisions.

Her tears fall again, not from guilt or shame, but from something just the opposite. She's grateful to feel something other than the cold emptiness that's been lodged in her soul for nearly two years. These tears are a sign that she's capable of feeling again. Stan was right when he said the rays of light in her painting represented hope. She is healing. Praise God.

CHAPTER 17

The next day *Statesman's* headline:

MONEY POURS INTO WRIGHT'S ELECTION CAMPAIGN FUND

Senator Richard Wright continues to amass a pile of political cash as new donations pour in just weeks before the citizens of Texas vote. Perhaps more telling is that Wright's political committee and campaign are sitting on close to $20 million, according to finance reports filed at the Texas Division of Elections. Last evening, Wright, diligent on the campaign trail, attended a dedication ceremony for The Matthew Horse Therapy Center, then spoke candidly with locals at Willy's bar until closing.

After reading the highlighted front-page article, she frantically searches through the rest of the newspaper for any mention of the horse center dedication or, more importantly, Brett Matthews's legacy. She finds none, and the room feels like it's closing in on her. Her chest expands as her rage grows. Kristine Walker promised her an article. Not finding one, she crumbles the newspaper and throws it on the floor. The front-page article about Richard and his campaign money seems to hold more value than an article about helping others with a newly renovated therapy center and a few choice words about the good man who left this world too soon.

Hurling her coffee cup against the wall would give a voice to her anger, but she realizes that no good will come from it—not one single thing will change.

In addition to the lack of news reporting the dedication, her anger is fueled by Richard's behavior. First, he dodged any conversation with her during the dedication and only posed on demand for a photo. Then, he didn't come back to the ranch. Since her house is closer to the equine center and Willy's Bar than downtown, she thought he would join her here. An image of the limo pulling up to the horse center with Richard and Amanda reinforces her distrust. He could have sent Amanda back alone in the limo, but his absence this morning supports her theory that he cares a great deal for his campaign manager, and he's making a choice. She chews her nail, wondering how much of his behavior can be blamed on the pressure of the campaign. Making excuses to frame him in a better light tires her.

Engulfed in negativity, she vows to counteract it by thinking of three things she is grateful for. First, she's grateful that there are only two weeks until the election and an end to this craziness. Second, she's grateful for the dedication's success. In the absence of an article in today's paper, she'll pay a professional photographer and journalist, vowing to find a magazine that will feature The Matthews Horse Therapy Center. Third, she has her family—her beautiful son, her daddy, Stan, Jamie, and Rusty. She's lucky to have a family who loves her and this beautiful ranch to call home.

She dials Richard's number only to get an automated voicemail… *please leave a message.* She decides against that. There, she did her part as the concerned fiancé—she tried calling, and he'll see the missed call.

Checking her watch, she hurries to have breakfast at the main house with Jamie and her son. Jamie graciously left the equine center shortly after the dedication to relieve Lola, who needed to get back to college for an early morning class. Thoughts of sitting at the family table with Jamie and Matthew bring a smile that overshadows any woes of Richard.

"Good morning!" Gabby calls in a cheerful voice, entering the ranch house. Her heart knows she is home by the rich aroma of freshly baked biscuits, the sounds of laughter, and Matthew's cute baby talk.

"Hey," Stan says, looking up from taking a sip of his coffee. His face shines behind the swirling steam, and his smile reveals his enthusiastic spirit.

"Hey, a room filled with my favorite people." She hugs Jamie, then lowers to plant a kiss on her son. "Have you been a good boy for Jamie?"

She goes to sit, and Stan pushes his chair back from the table. "Where's mine? Don't I deserve some love?" His eyes sparkle.

She feels the heat rising to her face as Jamie watches. Not doing anything would raise suspicion. She's hugged and kissed Stan numerous times in the past. However, thinking of the act seems awkward after his declaration of love. Not waiting for her response, he stands, places his hands on her shoulders, and whispers in her ear before pecking her on the cheek. She blushes.

Out of the corner of her eye, she observes Jamie's reaction. Jamie, with a poker player's face, turns and diverts her attention to Matthew. Stan, aware of the older woman's focus on the child, brushes Gabby's neck with his lips before giving her a second kiss, then returns to his seat.

Damn, Stan is going to pursue this publicly. Her heart races as she runs her fingers through her hair. She's unable to look him in the eye and reaches for the coffee pot with a shaky hand.

No one would blame him. History reveals that waiting four years to get Gabby's attention hasn't worked.

He breaks the silence. "What are your plans for the day?" He raises his eyebrows and smiles like he holds a secret.

"I'm not sure. Maybe, since it's a beautiful fall day, Matthew and I will go for a walk. We'll go visit the horses and the cattle."

"I asked Suzanne to fill in for me at the horse center."

"Suzanne? I thought she left us to work at that other place."

"She quit that job, and since we expanded, we hired more help. With the dedication, I didn't bother to run it past you. I hope hiring her was okay?"

"Sure, she's wonderful. We're grateful to have her back. I'll let you handle the hiring. You know what is best."

"Great. Today, I'm working the ranch. You could help. We're separating the calves from their mothers. Your dad, Rusty, and me...it will be like old times."

He sees her eyes drop, knowing he's reminded her of Brett's absence. "You haven't ridden in a while. It would be fun to have you out there with us. Really, won't you consider it? Take Matthew out this morning for a walk, then after lunch, while he's down for his nap, ride Lady out to the north pasture. Jamie, will you watch Matthew this afternoon?"

Jamie nods. "He's right. You should do it. Matthew's no problem. I'd love to watch him."

She bites her lip, contemplating his offer. Being out in the pastures riding Lady is hard work, and in addition to connecting her with nature, she'll be exhausted, but that will keep her mind off her problems.

She slaps her hands on her thighs. "Okay. You're right. Lady and I could both use the exercise. Thanks, Jamie, for watching Matthew."

The older woman smiles. "It's my pleasure. I love having a little one around here again."

"Great!" Stan reaches for Gabby's hand and squeezes it.

When she gets to the barn, the new ranch hand who cleans the stalls and other daily jobs has Lady saddled. Stan must have sent the young man a text. Out of habit, Gabby fishes the apple from her pocket and leans into Lady's neck, patting her on her nose.

"Oh, how I've missed you." She hugs the mare.

Lady seems more interested in the apple in her hand than being loved. After untying the mare from the fence, Gabby slips her foot into the stirrup, grunting as she swings her leg over the horse's back. This task used to be effortless; now it's clear she needs to beef up her exercise routine or perhaps a gentle reminder that she should spend more days on the ranch.

The sun is warm, with only a few wispy clouds in the sky. She sits high in the saddle, taking in the clean air and the miles of land that reach out as far as she can see.

The main cattle drive took place last week, moving the herd into their new home for the winter months. She recalls the last time she helped with the cattle two years ago. It puts a smile on her face to think of her daddy and Rusty singing and humming as they led the herd. Brett, Stan and Ryder, and the other wranglers took up the back and the sides, making sure no stragglers were left behind. Since cattle move at a slow pace, a routine drive typically takes a few days. She recalls many fond memories.

Yes, Brett loved the time he spent on the ranch. Since he was a hard worker and a great horseman, she's certain she isn't the only one missing him today. She looks to the sky and hopes to find comfort in thinking he's looking down on her. Her spirit longs to feel his presence. Lord knows how much she misses him. A dragonfly flits past, reminding her of a Native American legend that tells of ancestors visiting through these gentle creatures. She closes her eyes in gratitude.

Tonight, she'll have company to share in the misery of missing someone because the bellowing will be relentless. The cows will miss their babies, and the calves will cry for their mothers. Though necessary in this business, it's difficult for both animals. Reminded of the strong maternal bond between a cow and her calf, her son, Matthew, comes forefront in her mind as she remembers the comfort she feels whenever he's in her arms.

She clicks her tongue against the roof of her mouth, commanding Lady to trot. After a minute, her body relaxes with the rhythmic movement, and she and Lady are in sync. As she nears the north pasture, King waves his Stetson in her direction. Stan is cutting a calf with Ryder's help. She smiles, remembering how hard he worked to attain this skill that requires intense horsemanship to separate a calf from the rest of the herd. She watches, feeling a connection to nature, her horse, and the ranch. Then she sits straighter in the saddle as her soul sings praise, happy to be home.

Even on this mid-October day, the sun's intense rays beat down, and Gabby wipes the sweat from her brow. Her throat is dry, and dust covers her boots. Her water bottle was drained nearly an hour ago. However, the good news is the job is done. Now separated from their mothers, the calves are herded to a pasture near the barn so the wranglers can keep a close eye on them since the youngsters can be easy prey for coyotes and bobcats.

King rides in close to his daughter. "How are you? You okay?"

"Hot. I forgot how warm the sun can be this late in October." She takes off her leather gloves and wipes her forehead. "But it's all good. I'll sleep tonight."

He tips his hat. "We finished in record time. Glad you decided to help. Proud of you. Just like the old days. I've missed you." He reaches for her hand. "I'll see you back at the barn. I got a little surprise planned." He winks.

What could her daddy be up to?

As she rides back to the barn, she mentally notes her chores, realizing that her workday isn't finished. First, there's Lady to water and feed, then brush before she can call her day over. She could assign these duties to the young ranch hand; however, she wishes to bond with Lady. On her way past the corral, hay bales form a circle around the fire pit, and wranglers hang close, talking with red solo cups in their hands. The Cooper Restaurant food truck parked in the lane suggests that something close to a hoedown is about to erupt. After these past few seasons following Brett's fatal accident, a celebration after a hard day's work seems highly appropriate. Her daddy's a smart man to thank the men for their grueling labor.

Turning the corner to the watering trough, a spray of water hits her from the side. Stan's robust laughter greets her.

"Stan Adams, how dare you?" She yells, wiping the water running from her chin.

She grabs the bucket next to the trough and runs after him, spilling what water remains. He stops, allowing her to drench him.

"Feels great." He's grinning. "That all you got?" Before she can react, he turns the hose on her again. A huge stream of water cascades over her.

She screams and commences the chase, grabbing the rubber hose and pinching it off until only dribbles of water seep from the nozzle he holds.

"That's not fair," he says with his hands on his hips.

"Sure, it is…after I was ambushed."

They both laugh, doubling over, failing to see the figure standing near the fence watching.

Marie's hands are crossed over her chest. "Really? A water fight? Both of you are acting like children."

"Hi. It's called cooling off after a hot day in the sun. You could join."

She declines his invitation and shakes her head.

"When did you get here?" He takes steps toward her.

"Apparently, not early enough. I need to talk with you, but this isn't the right time." She turns and stomps away.

Gabby wipes her hands on her shirt. "I'm sorry, Stan."

"For what…for having some fun?" He turns off the spigot.

"She's upset."

"Lately, she's always upset."

"Tonight's supposed to be a celebration. It's important to Daddy. Go talk to her. Let's have a nice evening."

"I guess you're right." He starts walking but then calls over his shoulder, "There are T-shirts from the state fair in the barn. They're clean, but most of all, they're dry."

The barbeque tastes great, and country music fills the air from the three-member band. A friendly but competitive game of horseshoes between her daddy and a few wranglers provides additional entertainment. She sits on a haybale next to Jamie, bouncing Matthew on her knee.

"This is the best day I've had in a while." Gabby wipes some smears of macaroni and cheese off her son's face.

"I'll second that. It's always a fine day when I'm not cooking dinner." Jamie laughs. "Since I got you alone, what's going on with you and Richard?"

"Not much. He didn't come home last night. No call from him today. He hardly ever asks about Matthew. I wish they would spend more time together." She combs through Matthew's hair with her fingers. "He's busy on the campaign."

"I've been hearing that excuse for months." The older woman pinches her lips as if she's holding back words. "What's going on with you and Stan?"

"Why?"

"Something's goin' on—remember who you're talking to. I've known you since you were a wee little one." She winks.

"It's complicated."

"Love usually is." Jamie looks up to the sky.

"While you were out this afternoon, Rita and Marie had words over tea on the porch. Mind you, I'm not one to eavesdrop and spread gossip…well, just enough." Jamie looks over her shoulder before continuing. "Seems like Miss Rita is getting impatient. From the bits and pieces of the conversation, Rita's pushing for Stan and Marie to get married."

Gabby's back straightens.

"Rita told her how nice the ranch is in early spring…with all the bluebonnets in bloom, the birds singing, and the temperatures not too hot. Says it's the most wonderful time of year for a gathering, perfect for a weddin.' She starts by talking about her own weddin' to your daddy. Then, she says, not to worry about a thing, that she would pay for everything, make it as simple or grand an affair as Marie wishes."

Gabby's eyes never waver from Jamie's. From Gabby's own experience, she knows Rita can be very persuasive.

"So how did Marie respond? Did she agree?"

"Said she'll think about it, but I could tell she seemed pretty keen on the idea." Jamie locks her elbows and places her hands on her thighs. "I ask myself, what would my dear friend, Anna, want for her daughter? You, child, are rooted in this land. From what I've seen, Stan's also found his place here. He's dug his boots in, and he's in deeper as time goes by. Everyone knew he was here to stay after he built his house. Rita had a part in that, too, mind you. You've got much to think about, sweet thing." Jamie squeezes her hand before leaving her seat. "I'm in your corner, like always. Time's not on your side. I'll go check on the caterer."

Gabby watches the slight hitch in Jamie's step as she contemplates the possibility of Stan's wedding. She taps her foot to the beat of the music, but her mind continues to focus on this new development. Surely, Stan is not aware of his mother's plan. Why does life have to be so complicated? Matthew snuggles into her chest as it's soon his bedtime. The sound of his gentle breathing is comforting, and she imagines what it would be like to be blissfully wrapped in innocence.

The fall evening temperatures drop quickly as the sun slips out of sight. A light breeze blows from the west. Gabby pulls the hay bale that serves as her seat closer to the fire and rubs Matthew's legs to keep them warm.

A figure emerges from the lengthening shadows. Rita approaches, holding a blanket. "Here, take this. Matthew could get a chill." Her stepmother wraps the fleece throw around her shoulders and tucks the ends around Matthew's legs.

"Thanks."

"You'll mind the cold more with those damp jeans. I sent Stan inside for dry clothes. Don't know what the two of you were thinking." Rita shifts her weight and clears her throat. "We need to talk."

From her tone, this is serious.

"Is something wrong?"

Rita's return stare sends chills down her spine that can't be blamed on the evening breeze. It's as if she should already know the obvious.

"It has pained me to watch Stan struggle these past few years. Now, with Marie, he finally has a chance for happiness. As a mother, you understand. You would want the same for Matthew." Rita nods toward the babe who sits in Gabby's lap.

"Stan loves looking at the stars, and as many as there are out to-night, I take that as an omen." She tilts back and looks up. Then, she lifts her beer to toast. "Tonight, I'm celebrating." She pulls her shoulders back. "Marie's wearing Stan's ring. We're all thrilled—your dad, me, and, of course, Stan." Her stare seems to penetrate as though wanting to catch a surprise reaction.

It takes serious concentration for Gabby not to blink, and she does her best to hold an emotionless gaze.

Rita takes another sip of her beer. "I'm asking you to be happy for him. Congratulate them. Be supportive."

"I thought they had differences to work through."

"You thought wrong. She's planning a spring wedding right here on the ranch. Just like mine to your dad. It will be wonderful for Stan."

Rita raises her eyebrows. Gabby kisses her little one and holds him a bit tighter.

"We've had so much heartache and rough times. Tonight is the first celebration of many for our whole family. Let's keep them com-ing."

Gabby bites the inside of her cheek.

"Hey, there you are." King stands in front of them. "I've come to claim my bride. Hear that country jam? This old man wants to dance." He takes Rita's hand and gives her a hug, lifting her off her feet.

Rita giggles and places her hands around his waist. "I was just telling Gabby about our good news—Stan and Marie's engagement. She's graciously agreed to help with the plans."

Under King's steady gaze, Gabby lowers her eyes and turns away.

Then she stands, gathering the blanket tightly around her son.

"You two go dance. Matthew needs his bed. Thanks, Daddy. All of this was a nice surprise."

Flashing a fake smile, she turns and purposefully slows her gait even though she wants to run screaming. Jamie warned her, but she wasn't prepared.

Walking past the corral, she sees that the ranch hands are gathered. Loud voices fill the air. Stan has his back to her, but Marie gives a hearty wave. Gabby pretends she doesn't see and quickens her pace.

Once inside her house, she rests her back against the closed front door and sighs in relief that she's alone. Her heart pounds, and she's baffled that her face is wet. It's puzzling that she's so emotional. How could her recent exchange with Stan create such a whirlwind of emotions? Rita's words play like a needle stuck in the groove of a warped vinyl record...*be happy for him, be supportive, help with the plans.* These words tumble over and over in her mind, and accompanying them is Rita's face.

Why am I so upset? Faking her feelings for Richard requires less effort than pretending she's happy for Stan and Marie.

Earlier tonight, Jamie asked two questions. First, *What is going on with you and Richard?* And second, *What is going on with you and Stan?* Was Jamie forcing her to acknowledge the truth? Her relationship with Richard has been like train cars derailing, one after another. Is she waiting for the domino effect that will guarantee a disaster?

Yesterday another truth came to light. She's been like a schoolgirl with her first crush ever since Stan professed his love. The only thing that will calm her angst is speaking with Stan. However, getting him alone tonight will take nothing short of a miracle. She's desperate to hear Stan's side of the story. Obviously, he hasn't told Marie that they're finished.

With sleep not coming, she stands at her window in the wee hours of the morning. Her eyes follow the lane to Stan's house. She knows they're in there together, in bed making love, and her gut rolls. She twirls the ring on her finger; what goes around comes around. How did this craziness come about? Up until now, her heart had only had room for Brett. Maybe she's lonely, and because she's low on Richard's priority list, she's becoming one of those needy women who need attention—someone she vowed never to be. But this current state of madness started with three little words sealed with a kiss, and it was magical. He meant it, and she felt it.

CHAPTER  18

The ringtone on her phone interrupts her late morning slumber.

"Hello?"

"Hey, Gab, you're coming back to town today, right? Right?"

She notes the sharpness in Richard's tone. "Is that a question or a demand?" She turns the clock so she can read the time...7:30 a.m.

"Can you be nice? Geez..."

"I was thinking the exact same thing. Let's have a do-over. How about starting with *good morning?*" She rubs her head and sits up in bed.

"Okay, good morning! There. You happy?"

She lets his sarcasm slide. Clearly, something's wrong. "Tell me what's going on."

"Amanda came down with the flu. She sounds terrible. Can't get out of bed. Of all the times to be sick. You need to get here ASAP. It's crunch time, and we're on the final countdown. Today of all days, I have a full schedule.

"Hey, I need to run. Get here as soon as you can. Check your e-mail as the schedule is there. I don't have time to coordinate now as…damn, I must get to my 8:00 a.m. I'll meet you at headquarters at 11:00 a.m.…the 11:30 meeting is critical. Bye."

Just like that…disconnected.

She swings her feet over the edge of the bed and shakes her head in rhythm to her inner dialogue: *How are you…I miss you…How's my son?* Yes, Richard is under stress. Yes, it is the final countdown to a brutal two-year campaign. But really, does that explain his abrupt behavior? She stands and stretches, reaching her hands to the ceiling in praise, an effort to ward off the negativity heavily weighing her down. *So, Amanda's sick. That's unfortunate. The result is that I move up on his priority list…he needs me. I would rather he want or miss me…or do I really just not care?*

The priority on her to-do list this morning is to see Stan. She's desperate to understand how his failed engagement turned into a spring wedding, a short twenty-four hours after he professed his love for her.

Instead of finding Stan, Gabby finds herself behind the wheel with Matthew in the back seat, driving to campaign headquarters. Before leaving the ranch, she had popped into the main house, hoping to catch Stan for an explanation, but he and Marie had gotten an early start to their workday at the equine center. She checks her watch. There's no time for a detour if she's to give Matthew to Lola before accompanying Richard to his meeting. In her haste, she hasn't checked his entire schedule to prepare for the busy afternoon.

She pushes Richard's dilemma into the background. The long drive back to the city gives her time to hypothesize about the situation with Stan, dreaming up every possible explanation for the recent chain of events. Was Stan drunk when he kissed her? Did he do it just to see her response? Was he proving a point? Is this a shotgun wedding because Marie is pregnant?

After contemplating each scenario, she arrives at this conclusion: Stan is the most honest, considerate man she has ever met. He's not vindictive or manipulative. Certainly, he would never be coerced into doing something, even if the influencer was his mother. There must be a logical explanation, and that reason, whatever it may be, needs to come directly from him, "from the horse's mouth"—a phrase her daddy is known to say.

However, whatever it is that's changed, a confrontation with Stan will have to wait. She will be late if she doesn't push the gas pedal a bit harder. Memories of Brandon, Brett's twin, and their laps on the F1 track pop into play as she speeds along. Men—Stan, Richard, and the mysterious Brandon Matthews—no wonder she's on edge. She needs a female voice to add perspective and understanding. She needs her best friend, Ella. Ever since Ella married Stan's brother, Will, and moved to Washington, D.C., three years ago, their friendship has waned. She voice-activates her phone. What did a girl do before cellular phones?

"Hello, Ella!" Her voice is bright and cheery. "How are you and my precious goddaughter, Gracie?"

"Hey, it's good to hear your voice. I just hung up with Rita. Will is trying to move his meetings around so we can be there."

"Be here when?"

"This weekend for the engagement party." The line goes silent. "Surely, you knew. I'm not letting the cat out of the bag again, am I?"

Gabby's stomach flips, and she bites her lip.

"Oh dear, from your silence, I gather that you don't know. Rita didn't say that it was a surprise."

"They made an announcement last evening. The party this weekend is the surprise."

"From what Rita said, it's not a big Texas-sized party; it's a small, family thing because she wants Will to be there since he'll be Stan's best man. This way, we can get to know Marie better before the big day."

"The big day?"

"The wedding day, silly. The first Saturday in April. Girlfriend, get it on your calendar. Little Matthew must have his mama sleep deprived. Gabby, what's going on? You're acting weird."

"Sorry, things have been strange and confusing, and I don't know where to start."

"Gab, I'm grabbing a second cup of Joe, so fill me in. Gracie's at a play date, so you have my undivided attention."

"First, Mr. Brandon Matthews keeps showing up. It's a bit creepy because he looks so much like Brett. I thought I was going to faint the first time we met. He's always there—kind of shows up unexpectantly. He came to the dedication of the horse center. Every time he's near, it's surreal, and when he touches me…"

"Whoa, when he touches you?" Her tone sounds as if she's surprised.

"Nothing sexual. We danced…at the dedication. I can barely look at him, Ella. Dancing with him was so unnerving. The flood of emotions was overwhelming." Gabby swerves the car to avoid vultures picking at a fresh carcass on the country road.

"I'm sorry we couldn't be there. You know I would have. Where are you now? It sounds like you're in a car."

"Driving back to town to meet Richard. Amanda is sick, so I get the chance to fill in for her. Lucky me."

"Is that sarcasm I detect? This is what you and Richard have been planning all your lives—like forever. This is the big time. A few weeks to go, and you get to be the next Mrs. Governor. That is so exciting. Oh my God, my best friend, the first lady! Our sorority picked you as most likely to succeed, and you are living up to that title. I can't wait for our yearly sisters' luncheon held in the governor's mansion. So awesome. So Gabby-like!"

"Hold on there, Ella. Richard still has to win the election."

"He will. All the polls have him winning over Green by more than 20 percent. It's a given. I'll help you plan your parties and your wardrobe. Whatever you need."

"Amanda has all of the parties planned, and Daddy took me on a shopping spree months ago. But thanks for the offer."

"So, I don't get it. You're living the life that many can only imagine, and it's the life that you once dreamed of. You should be on a high. What's the problem?" Ella finally pauses, and the silence is uncomfortable. "Gabby, fess up! This is me, Ella."

"It's Richard." She bites the inside of her cheek. "No, that's not fair." She takes a deep breath. "It's me. I don't think this is what I want. It's what Richard wants. It's what Daddy wants. But me, I'm not so sure."

"You're tired. It's been a long, tough journey. You need a break. After the election, you and Richard can get away and spend time with each other."

"Richard hasn't spent any time with Matthew or me in weeks—make that months."

"He's really busy. Surely, you can understand that."

"Amanda loves him. She told me."

"Amanda...the campaign lady? Shut up! When?"

"A few weeks ago. They're together every day and most nights. They slept together before, and I think they are sleeping together now."

"Before doesn't count. You were pregnant with Brett's baby. You can't blame Richard for that relationship or for not spending more time with Matthew."

She's taken aback by the words of the big lie. Ella doesn't know that Matthew is Richard's son. The cover-up was so successful and keenly orchestrated that even her best friend doesn't grasp the lie Gabby lives daily. Could it be that Gabby's authentic self is buried so deeply that living the lie has caused her to lose her way?

Ella must have taken a sip of her coffee during the brief silence because she hears the clink of a cup on a saucer. "Most powerful men have mistresses. Look at JFK, Clinton—even Martin Luther King. After Richard wins, he'll be more careful. He must be careful now if what you say is true because the tabloids haven't printed anything."

"No, they haven't. I think that's because Daddy pays them not to print."

"Richard has always had a wandering eye. You've always known, Gabby."

"I thought he had changed. I thought that he had learned from the past and wanted us to work. I need to believe that."

"Oh, honey, I'm sorry. However, need I remind you that everything in life has a tradeoff. So, there's been a little infidelity. If he's elected governor, it's bound to happen again. Women will be after him; it's the way of the world."

"What if Will had a little infidelity? You would understand, right?"

"I would kill him. Just sayin.' However, Will is not going to be the next Texas Governor. Look ahead, Gabby. After your years in Texas, the White House could be next. Remember the Bushes? You could be the next Laura Bush!"

"Ella, I don't love Richard. I'm living a lie. Get it." She's practically screaming into the phone. Matthew stirs at her outburst and starts to whimper. "I'm sorry, that was uncalled for. Now you'll understand. After Richard wins, I'll be committing for four years, eight years, or even longer. I want to have love in my life. I want that for Matthew and for me more than being first lady."

"Then you have to break off your engagement. If you feel that strongly about it, the solution is obvious. Better now than later."

"That's exactly what Amanda said."

"So why haven't you? Of course, King wants you there. He's been leading you and Richard around as if you have nose rings."

"My God, Ella."

"We're being honest. That's what best friends are for. Gabby, you're smart. You played the game, and you played it convincingly. Texas will love you. I thought this was what you wanted. You've never said anything different. It's shocking to have you tell me this now. I thought we were best friends and family as well."

"There is so much you don't know. I really want to tell you everything, starting from the beginning, but I can't now." Her angry tone dissipates and is replaced with one that conveys sadness. "I'm on a time crunch. Hey, I'm here at headquarters, and I need to run. Next weekend, we'll have some time alone, and we can finish this conversation. Deal?"

"Okay, promise? I miss our talks. I miss you."

Gabby parks in the loading zone in front of the old bank building. The plan is for Lola to meet her here, get Matthew, and take the car back to the condo. With no signs of Lola, Gabby grabs her son from his car seat and proceeds up the stairs. She greets Tom and adds, "Don't let them tow the car."

Inside campaign headquarters, volunteers are bustling with excitement as they fold pamphlets. Boxes are piled high. She still hasn't checked the schedule. What is happening this afternoon? She searches the room for Richard and finds her daddy.

"Hey, Daddy, I got here as soon as I could." She leans in to peck him on the cheek. "What's going on?"

He looks at her and arches his brow. "The practice run for the F1 race. We're doing the start, complete with a photo shoot. You and Richard will be on the track. He's the starter. Where's your blue? You're supposed to wear blue, the Mercedes team color."

Her eyes follow down her outfit, her ivory top and tan skirt. "I didn't know."

"There's no time for shopping. Amanda has clothes in the back. Change into something trendy, and make sure it's blue." He reaches his arms out to Matthew. "Come to Gramps. Your mama needs to get changed into something *blue*." He shakes his head as if she's a forgetful child.

Gabby hands over her son and rolls her eyes.

"Better hurry. Time's a wastin,'" King says with urgency.

She's quick to get to the back closet, where Amanda keeps more clothes than the average woman could possibly afford. She rummages through the rack, pulling out whatever is blue. There are three dresses.

"Good, I have choices." She holds each one up for inspection in the mirror hanging on the back of the door and disqualifies the sequined one. This is a car race, not a cocktail party.

She strips and shimmies into the light-blue silk. Her bra shows since it's cut low. Forgoing the bra isn't an option because the silk clings. She bites her lip, holding up the last blue dress. It's a medium shade of blue chiffon with small cap sleeves. She avoided it initially because it's the shortest of the three. And that's a problem because Gabby is four inches taller than Amanda. With no time to waste, Gabby pulls the dress over her head and checks her image in the mirror. The dress fits, and the high-cut bodice covers her bra. Her eyes smile until they track down to her thighs. She hasn't shown this much leg since college. Bending over could be a problem. She'll need to be careful, but she has no other options. This will have to do.

Now for shoes. Amanda wears very stylish shoes with high heels, and the selection is plentiful. Since Amanda models on the side and most models buy their shoes a size bigger, that should work in her favor. Gabby picks several with an open heel, regardless of color, except for white. Even in Texas, no proper lady wears white after Labor Day. Her heel will hang over the back, but that's how it's going to be. The first three pairs she tries make her feel like she's Cinderella's evil stepsister stuffing her foot into the tiny glass slipper. The tan Jimmy Choos are doable—not perfect, and she's already preparing for blisters. Maybe the shoot will be quick, and she can slide the shoes off when she's seated at the grandstand. No one will be the wiser.

There's a knock on the door. It's Richard. "Gabby, Lola's here. You need to give her instructions. Leaving in five. Gabby?"

"Yes, I'm getting dressed."

"Your dad told me. I explicitly instructed you to check the schedule. I'm sure it said to wear blue."

"I know. I'm sorry. I didn't have time."

She hears him walk away, imagining the disapproving scowl he's probably wearing. After another glimpse in the mirror to view her transformation, she bends over at the waist, shakes her head, then stands, straightening her hair by running her fingers through the sides. She pinches her cheeks for color. The dress is not her usual style—this time, the cameras will be capturing a diva. *Thank you, Amanda.* The rule to dress conservatively just flew out the window. She's certain to turn heads.

She's quick to notice Richard's double take when he first lays eyes on her. He immediately walks toward her, grins, and reaches for a hug and kiss. "Wow, you look fantastic," he whispers in her ear, the nicest words they have exchanged in weeks.

She closes her eyes. *I am the same person. Men are so visual.* It's like she controls the room with the stares and smiles she's receiving. *Play the part, Gabby. You've been on the stage for months. This is just another act.* She's amazed but also ashamed that she feels so empowered by the influence she seems to have. Is this how Richard feels whenever he faces the public? It must be hard for him not to succumb. Is this the high that builds the ego and contributes to the fall of many influential politicians and celebrities? The revelation brings clarity about the future she will have as the governor's wife.

CHAPTER 19

Moments later, their black limo drives from the city, past the airport to the F1 track. Gabby rides, sitting next to Richard with King and Rita opposite them. Few words are spoken as Richard mentally rehearses his speech.

As they approach the gate to the racetrack, the size of the crowd amazes Gabby. Then again, she wonders how many are attending using the free tickets distributed by Steven Prime, her daddy, and those bought from the millions in the campaign fund. Another part of the political game—the marketing and advertising. It is too naive to believe that the candidate is elected on his own merit and platform.

She pulls her dress down a few millimeters and plans how she'll step out of the limo in a ladylike fashion. As the limo reaches the front entrance, it slows to a halt. It's showtime.

The driver opens their door, and the reporters are quick to push in close, and the cameras click. Richard exits the car and waves, then turns to take her hand and lifts her in a manner that requires little effort on her part. For that, she is thankful, as she uses her left hand to keep her dress straight. She looks up to Richard, viewing him differently—not as the distant father or uncaring lover, but as the candidate for governor. His suit is perfectly tailored and pressed. Every hair is in place as he extends a smile from his handsome face that will burn a lasting impression in everyone's memory. He's all that and more. The crowd cheers as if he's the biggest rock star in the world. This is not what she expected.

Reality brings her to focus on her job from the book of rules—*smile, Gabby, show energy, and wave.* Work the crowd. Make them feel like you're their best friend. Be glad they are here. Shake hands and chitchat. *We are on the last lap to bring home the gold.*

When Richard campaigned this past summer, King, Rita, and Amanda shared in the journey since she was still grieving Brett and taking care of her newborn. With the election getting closer and the daily exposure, Richard's popularity has grown to unprecedented levels. Both Lola and Ella mentioned his lead ranking in the polls, but she never considered the value of those numbers. As she created distance these past few weeks by removing herself from the campaign to deal with the dedication of the horse center, she hasn't contemplated the magnitude of Richard's current status. Her fiancé is a celebrity.

She looks over her shoulder to King. He's equally engaging with the people—smiling, patting men's backs, shaking hands. He seems lighter and brighter than she's seen him in a while. She watches him introduce Rita, who is proud to hang on his elbow.

Richard answers a few of the reporter's questions, then turns, flashes his perfect smile with a sparkle in his eyes, and encircles her waist with her arm.

A yell from the crowd exclaims, "Kiss her. One for the camera!"

His lips touch hers, and the cheering crowd encourages the moment. The impromptu peck turns into a passionate kiss. Upon his release, the clicking cameras sound like applause. Then, something short of magic transpires, and her cold heart melts. She catches her breath to calm the barrage of sensations. Maybe there is a connection between them. Maybe the pressure of the election is creating distance in their relationship. Maybe they do have a future.

Next, security guards open a path, ushering them into the inner building, restricting attendance to only those with VIP tickets. Once inside, Steven Prime approaches with a wide grin. "That was the kind of reception I like to see. Caught it all live, here on the TV." He shakes hands with King and Rita and pats Richard's back. He takes Gabby's hands in his, closes in for a kiss, and whispers in her ear, "You are an angel—the bright star that brings him light."

His remark generates a heat that rises from her chest to her face. Her smile radiates as if acknowledging that she agrees.

Immediately she senses she's being watched. Following her instincts, she turns, locking eyes with a familiar pair as they shamelessly travel from her head to her feet and then reverse until their eyes meet. He smiles and grins as though he has undressed her. Feeling vulnerable and exposed, she shuts her eyes as her heart pounds and little beads of perspiration form on her lip.

Gabby can tell by his grin that Brandon Matthews relishes his ability to brazenly unnerve her to her core. He keeps a distance but continues the unspoken dialogue. Is his plea to get to know his family sincere, or does he want something more?

In an instant, a hand grabs her and pulls her toward the grandstand's private tunnel leading to the track. As they exit the tunnel, tripods with campaign posters of her freedom painting stand next to the temporary stage with the F1 Championship trophy and a podium.

An employee in a blue suit and wearing a badge guides her to the stage. She squints in the bright Texas sun, facing hundreds of fans in the grandstand. The Mercedes F1 team—the owner, two drivers, and mechanics, along with Steven Prime—join them.

After the opening welcome and introductions, Richard takes the podium. She stands behind him, wishing she could cover her ears to dampen the thunderous applause. Richard waves to the cheering crowd, encouraging them even more. He stands tall, delivering his speech with a strong voice. His words echo in the space, and he exudes confidence, supporting the slogan *Richard Wright is the Right Choice.* The crowd roars.

Following his speech, the stage is dismantled while the cars roll to their starting positions for the practice run. Steven Prime hands her a set of earplugs and signals her to follow him to the side of the track. Richard stands front and center and is given headphones and a checkered flag. Engines rev as the drivers focus on the starting lights. As the fifth light flashes red, Richard waves the flag to signal the start of the race. Energetic shouts from the stands accompany the roar of the cars as they accelerate to round the first turn. Experiencing this level of excitement for the practice run, Gabby marvels at thoughts of the actual race.

Another tap on her shoulder steers her toward the paddock, the small area near the track where race cars are kept with space for mechanics to work. She follows without hesitation, assuming it is another Mercedes team member. When he turns to face her, her eyes open wide upon discovering that her escort is Brandon. His finger points to the entrance to the exclusive F1 Paddock Club.

"Hi," she says with a smile before remembering that they are both wearing earplugs. Thinking they can start a conversation is lame.

First, he nods, then, after bowing, makes a quick exit when she's within feet of Richard. Several men in the group have their heads turned to the television with its close-up views of the race. King and Prime are among them. She stands by Richard, even though she'd rather chat with Brandon, but notices that since leaving her side, he's seated in front of a computer at a table with his team. The earlier jovial mood changes to something more serious. Inside the Mercedes team paddock, they await the outcome, and their driver is holding a steady lead. This is the first practice race, and a second will run in a few hours. However, the qualifying round tomorrow will determine their car's position on the grid for race day.

Moving to the hallway of the F1 Paddock Club for quiet and privacy, she calls Stan, but the call promptly goes to voice mail, and she hangs up without leaving a message. Feigning interest in the car race, she surveys her surroundings before discreetly checking her e-mails. She opens the one with *campaign schedule* in the subject. There, in bold print, for today's F1 practice race, the text clearly states WEAR BLUE. She notices that the campaign schedule is packed, showing two and three events every day this week, including the F1 race this Sunday. If Richard expects her to be by his side, she'll need to coordinate this new schedule with Lola. She shakes her head. None of this was her plan. She should be at the ranch, getting things straight with Stan. Hadn't Ella mentioned an engagement party? She rubs the back of her neck.

"Hey, everything okay?"

She jumps.

"Sorry, I didn't mean to startle you. I noticed you left." Brandon flashes a wide smile. "We're not boring you, are we?"

"I'm sorry. No, not bored at all." She hopes her return smile is genuine. Looking at Brandon's face is still creepy, but at least it doesn't throw her into a coronary like when they met at the Foundation Room. "Just checking Richard's schedule. The campaign manager is sick, so I'll need to pick up her duties."

"Would that be Amanda?"

"You know her?"

"From the dedication." He beams.

"That's right. A group of you went to the bar."

"Amanda's not someone easily forgotten. Richard seems to enjoy her company." He raises an eyebrow. "Wish you would have joined us that night. It was fun. Gabby, I'm serious about getting to know my brother's family. When do I get to meet my nephew?"

"Seriously, please accept my apologies. Things have been crazy. And now, with Amanda sick..."

"I understand. Speaking of schedules after the race, at the end of the month, I'll be going with the team to Mexico for our race there." He looks down at his shoe. "Then we'll be off the first week in November before leaving again for Brazil. I can be back for the election. You can call and tell me where to find you." He shifts his weight and stares. "I'd really like that. Is that good with you?"

She shrugs her shoulders. "Okay, that would be fine, I guess. But I don't have your contact information."

His smile is wide. "And I don't have your phone number either. Let's take care of that now."

CHAPTER 20

At the small, local airport the next morning, Gabby leans on the fence and squints in the bright midmorning sun. She skipped the University Club's political luncheon so she could greet her visitors. When the King Air rolls to a stop, she opens the gate and runs, waving. Ella exits first with Gracie in her arms, followed by Will, Stan's brother.

"Hello, girlfriend! I've missed you." She embraces her best friend in a big hug. "It seems like forever since I've seen you. And look at you, Gracie. Do you remember me, Aunt Gabby?"

The toddler smiles, then buries her face in her mother's arm.

Ella steps back. "She'll warm up in time." She hugs her daughter. "Gabby, you're radiant. I know from our chat you're not much for campaigning, but campaigning looks good on you. Just one more week to go. It's so exciting."

Ella's off-handed remark causes Gabby to pause. Her joy in seeing her best friend claims rights to her happiness, not Richard's campaign.

Recently, thoughts of the campaign, combined with Stan and Marie's rushed engagement, turn over in her mind like a hamster on an exercise wheel. It's driving her crazy. Ella's visit is the perfect distraction.

Next, Will joins the group, loaded down with their luggage.

"Gabby, nice to see you. I expected to be chauffeured by my brother. Is he too lazy to give his bro a proper welcome?"

She laughs. "Hardly. It seems that Stan is the only one working these days. I've been slacking off, leaving him to do double duty at the equine center. This week Amanda, our campaign manager, got the flu and left me with the entire campaign schedule. But it's all good. I'm so happy you're here!" She clasps her hands together.

Will scans the area. "Where's Matthew?"

"Matthew is at the ranch with Jamie and Lola, his babysitter. She's wonderful with him. You'll meet her today."

Gabby signals good-bye to the pilot before taking a suitcase from Will to lighten his load.

"If you're ready, let's get on the road." She checks her watch. "We'll have time to go by the horse center and see Stan. With the new signage and renovations completed, the center looks great. I'm excited to show it to you."

"Marie's there too, right?" Ella asks.

She lowers her eyes. "Of course."

Stan sits on the porch of the Matthews Horse Therapy Center as Gabby's SUV pulls into the small parking lot.

Will runs to greet Stan. "Hey, bro, this is you working? I should have known it was all lies." He slaps Stan on the back before giving him a warm embrace. "Congratulations on your engagement. It's about time the old dog decided to settle down."

Stan looks from his brother to Gabby. Gabby bites her upper lip.

"Come on in. Marie's working with a client, but she'll be finished in a few."

Gabby hangs back, allowing Ella, Gracie, and Will to go through the front door first.

Gabby pulls on Stan's shirt. "Engagement. You're still going along with this? You told me..."

He shakes his head. "It's a long story. We'll talk later."

"Are you going through with this?"

"I can explain. We'll talk later."

"Stan..."

His brow knits, and his harsh stare stops her in her tracks before he nudges her through the doorway. "Later," he whispers in a stern tone.

She had visions that he would be all smiles when they met. This coldness is a surprise, and her heart sinks.

Inside the center, Gabby's cowboy painting quickly becomes the center of conversation.

"Wow, this is magnificent. Your painting skills are improving. You certainly captured Brett's likeness. I know how much you loved him," Ella says as she rubs Gabby's back. "As first lady, your sales will go through the roof with every Texan vying for one of your paintings." Then she jumps up and down. "But wait, think about this fascinating newspaper headline." She motions with her hand as if writing in the air. "First Lady Dumps Governor Wright After Reportedly Dead Husband Comes Back to Life."

Gabby turns away. Stan and Will stare at Ella, whose history of impulsive behavior includes an insensitivity that wounds others when she speaks without thinking.

Will is the first to break the uncomfortable silence. "Ella."

"What? If the twin looks like Brett, it's not impossible. I'm saying what everyone is thinking, right? When do I get to meet this Brandon guy?"

"Ella…" Will scolds his wife.

Gabby swallows the hard lump in her throat, and just like in their college days, she rescues her friend. "No harm done. It's true that seeing Brandon is unsettling because of his strong resemblance to Brett. Believe me, it stops there. We're just family." She rolls back her shoulders, takes a deep breath, and forces her best smile. "You'll meet him soon enough."

Stan glances at Gabby as though trying to read her thoughts.

Helping to advance from the awkward moment, Gracie toddles back to her dad and points to the horse in the corral. Will gladly cuddles his daughter. "Yes, let's go see the horses. Shall we?" They walk toward the door leading to the corral.

Ella looks at her as if to say sorry, and Gabby pats her friend's back to reassure her that all's well.

The small group approaches the corral as Marie helps her client dismount using the mounting block. Her client, Dave, has been receiving therapy to help him recover from a stroke. He continues to lean slightly to the right, and his foot drags, but his remarkable improvement after a few weeks has been uplifting for him and the staff.

After dismounting, he sits on the top of the mounting block and shifts to the side without steps. Marie pushes the walker close to help him stand. The client's face beams as he nuzzles the horse's neck and offers a carrot as a reward.

"This is what we do here...improve people's lives. It's addicting." Stan pulls his shoulders back, and Marie, with her small stature, fits under his armpit.

"I'm so glad you were free on such short notice to help us celebrate our engagement." She snuggles into Stan and extends her left hand for Will and Ella to inspect her engagement ring. A flush of green runs through Gabby's veins.

Then, Stan excuses himself to assist Dave to the van waiting to transport him back to the assisted living center, leaving them to chat with Marie.

Ella's hands are on her hips. "This quick engagement party came as a surprise. Makes me wonder if it's a shotgun wedding."

Marie gives a high-pitched laugh. "Nope, no one is holding a gun, and I'll share that I'm not pregnant. Stan asked me months back, and I'm the one who hesitated. But now, the timing seems right." Marie's glare forces Gabby to avert her eyes. Her tone implies she's settling a score.

Gabby accepts the challenge. "Tell us, what changed? The age difference will never go away, and Stan will never be the guy closing the bar."

Marie crosses her arms in front of her chest and turns to face her. "We had a long chat in bed one night, and let's just say we negotiated." She smiles. "Whoa, I've said too much. Come, let's visit the stables. I want to introduce you to Greg, our resident veteran."

The small troupe follows Marie.

"You go ahead. I need to follow up on some phone calls." Gabby waves before returning to the horse center.

Back in the office, she watches through the front window as Stan helps Dave sit in the van before he stows the walker in the back and converses with the driver. She's reminded that Stan is a solid man with high morals and integrity, so what is really going on? She's certain that Rita has played a role, but it's odd that Stan would make a huge commitment based on his mother's desires. Does Marie know of Stan's true feelings? How can Marie be at peace with their engagement?

Gabby walks out to the porch and sits on the glider. Her conversation with Stan is overdue. Stan waves as the van pulls away and strides toward the equine center.

"Where's Will and Ella?"

"Marie's giving them a tour. Gracie's curious about the horses." She stands. "I'm so confused. You're still engaged—how did that happen?"

"It's complicated."

"Damn right it is. I thought we had something. I thought…"

"We have something? Exactly what do we have? I'm all ears." He stands directly in front of her.

"You kissed me. You told me you loved me." Her eyes search his face for further explanation.

"That's right. I did kiss you, and I did tell you that I loved you." He stands a bit closer.

"What did you do with that information?"

Silence.

"Yes, nothing. You did nothing. You didn't say *I love you*. Nothing."

"That's not true. I kissed you back. I need time to figure this out."

"You've had nothing but time. First, there was Richard. Then there was Brett, and then lo and behold, you run back to Richard before Brett's in the grave. And now, you're still with Richard. I watch the news and read the papers, seems like your relationship is blooming."

"That's not fair."

"It may not be fair, but it's true. And let's add another to the list…Mr. Brandon, Brett's perfect twin. Is he in line ahead of me? I've waited and waited. Mother thinks that you play me. Marie thinks the same. Do you know what they say? Poor Stan, poor, poor Stan. Can you imagine how that makes me feel?

"Whenever you need something, who do you call? Yep, call Stan because he'll drop everything for you. Yes, I'm presently committed to marrying Marie. I want you to hear this from me. Okay? I'm not going to back away from my relationship with Marie to find that you have no intention of ever being with me." He holds her chin and stares into her eyes. "Tell me you love me. Break your engagement with Richard. I'll marry you tomorrow. I love you. I love Matthew."

Silence.

She rubs her forehead. "Wait, that means Marie knows she's your second choice, and she's fine with that?"

"Marie's no dummy. She negotiated—a million dollars if I walk or a million as a present on our wedding day."

Gabby's mouth opens. "You're staying with a girl who's in a relationship with you because of money? Now, I've heard it all. That's crazy. Why would you ever consent to that?"

"Most might agree, and others would say my love for you is crazy. Crazy versus crazy, Gabby."

She looks away and bites her lip.

"She picked April for the wedding. I'm through putting my life on hold while I watch your life's drama unfold. I'm moving forward with or without you, sweetheart. It's your choice." He tips his hat, steps to the side, and opens the door, leaving her alone on the porch.

Still turning over their conversation in her mind, she tries to gain perspective. Her feet weigh heavy, and her heart aches after hearing that Stan blames her for his years of unhappiness. It's true that over the past four years, she has leaned on him. He's been a rock, and she's forever grateful, but he's family, and that's what family does for one another. She has never purposefully taken advantage of his good graces. However, since he professed his love, their relationship has quickly turned upside-down. It's burdensome being told that she holds Stan's future in her hands. That, combined with Marie negotiating a marriage deal, is ridiculous. She can't even fathom why Stan would agree to such an arrangement. Someone with objectivity needs to intervene. Maybe it's time for a heart-to-heart chat with Daddy.

Swinging on the glider, she scratches her head, putting this information into the proper perspective. *According to Stan, Marie gains a million dollars regardless of my decision.* The only thing riding on her decision is Stan. His wedding is planned for spring; surely, she can sort out her life before then.

CHAPTER 21

B ack on her front porch at the ranch in the late afternoon, the sun sparkles like diamonds on the lake. The freshly cut fields with their stubble combined with comfortable temperatures alert that fall has arrived. Gabby gathers Matthew in her arms and wipes the small dirt smudge that he managed to get on his outfit from crawling on the wooden porch. She has been teaching him to say "Mama." When his sweet little voice sounds close to this, her heart swells. No one can possibly describe these joys of parenthood. She looks to the sky in gratefulness.

Earlier, it was decided that Ella, Will, and little Gracie would stay with Stan and Marie for the weekend. About thirty minutes ago, the foursome walked the lane to the main house, and Gabby sent Lola to join them. Lola graciously agreed to babysit this busy weekend at the ranch. Gabby sighs, checking her watch, a reminder that she's procrastinated long enough. It's time to gather her son and walk to the main house for the engagement party.

Today, Richard's schedule included attendance at the racetrack for the F1 qualifying round, so it's doubtful he'll make the trip to participate in the King family gathering. Since Amanda's speedy recovery and the election in ten days, Gabby can't find fault, and over the phone, he expressed his desire for her to be by his side. By saying yes to his request, she would have a viable excuse for her absence at the engagement celebration and a diversion from this inner turmoil.

A voice coming from the lane breaks her thoughts.

"Hello there."

"Jamie, this is a surprise. I thought you would be in the kitchen."

"My work is done for now. Besides, I needed a break. That woman is driving me crazy."

"That woman must be Rita?"

"Hovering over me supervising. It's like this party has been her entire life's goal. I shouldn't be complaining. I came to see you. I'm worried."

Jamie, a little short of breath, comes up the stairs and sits on the porch. "You picked the best spot on the ranch for your house. The view's beautiful from here."

Gabby knows she can confide in the woman who has known her since she was a child.

"You're right; I am a bit concerned. The celebration of Stan and Marie's engagement is bittersweet. Do you think they belong together?"

"You have been the love of Stan's life for a while now. I've sat and watched." Jamie rocks back and forth. "Marie…is she genuinely happy, or is she settling? I can't say for certain. Money is a great motivator; many have done more unethical things for much less."

Gabby's eyes open wide. "You know about their arrangement?"

"I'm probably not supposed to, but I keep my ears open."

"It's ludicrous, this prenuptial agreement. Has Daddy played a role…was it his idea? Does he know?"

"I can't say." Jamie pinches her lips together like she's hiding information.

Gabby shifts Matthew's weight on her lap. "Maybe this evening, I can lure Daddy into his office, share some GB Cowboy bourbon, and have a heart-to-heart."

Jamie takes her hand. "I'm going to speak to you as if you were my daughter. It really doesn't matter who knows what or what arrangements have been made or what your daddy wants. I understand the influence he has had on you. Since Anna died, he needs to protect you and guide you. The big question to answer is, what do *you* want? I care about you, and I care about Stan. I am asking you to follow your heart. Make your own decision." She slaps her hands down on her thighs. "There, I said what I came to say." Jamie stands and gives Matthew a kiss. "I'll see you soon. I have a special surprise for you, young man."

Gabby watches as the older woman heads toward the main house from where she came. Gabby wishes for a crystal ball. She wants the best for Stan, and the thought of breaking his heart is unbearable. She's suffering from doubt and fear due to the disastrous outcomes of some of her past choices. Can she trust her judgment now?

Attempting to discreetly approach this situation from a different angle, Gabby asked Lola to observe the engaged couple and report her professional opinion. As a psychology major, Lola may also unveil Gabby's secret, but the risk outweighs the payout.

All in all, she's certain the night will be memorable. She closes her eyes and prays for guidance. Upon opening them, the evening star appears right over Stan's house. Is this a sign? Stan's love isn't the problem; the predicament rests with her. Can she change her attitude from one of platonic love to romance? In their brief encounter, a spark ignited, but will that continue to fan into a passionate fire? She experienced that love with Brett, and expecting that level of love again might set the measuring stick too high.

To love or not to love is only a small part of the equation. There are many variables—all the people and circumstances involved in her decision. Jamie's advice to think only of herself proves selfish. The factors in the equation change over and over—Richard's career with her daddy's commitment and the opportunity to do good for the citizens of Texas. Then there is Stan and Marie's relationship. Marie—so young—but is she wise beyond her years? Gabby rationalizes that the promise of a million-dollar Band-Aid will suffice, covering any damage if the "arranged" marriage ends. The main concern is Stan since his mother already blames Gabby for the setbacks in his life. Lola's expert evaluation of the lovebirds will prove invaluable.

After placing Matthew in his stroller, she checks her profile in the mirror. On the outside, she looks confident and ready to face the world. Inside, she is not. Her stomach turns, and her head aches from wavering back and forth. Should she pluck petals off a daisy...does she, or doesn't she? In the past, a canvas and brush have solved many dilemmas. Could painting provide the answer?

Gabby is greeted by laughter as she and Matthew enter the ranch house where the rest of the family is gathered. It's as though her daddy's performing because all eyes are on him, allowing her to slip into the room unnoticed. His commanding voice engages the others as he elaborates on a verbal exchange at the racetrack. It seems his story centers on the various race car team members talking smack in an effort to intimidate.

Observing the audience, she notes that Ella and Will are snuggled on the couch, Rita holds Gracie, and Lola sits next to Marie, their knees almost touching. As she scrutinizes the younger women—Lola and Marie, Gabby feels her forehead for wrinkles. Compared to their innocence, she's survived more tragedies than they can imagine. Neither has said good-bye to her dead baby cradled in her arms. Neither has cared for her brain-dead husband, fully aware that his inevitable demise means all-encompassing grief. On the other end of the spectrum, neither has experienced the glories of marriage nor has given birth to a new life. Her life has been rich in both the good and the bad, and Stan has been there through most of it. She's amazed that he's willing to share her life and love her despite the baggage, but perhaps it's these moments that have formed their bond.

A presence behind her causes her to jump.

Stan squeezes her elbow. "I've missed you."

"Hey. Daddy is on a roll."

He kisses her cheek. "He likes playing up to a new and bigger audience. Here, give me Matthew. He's getting so big, your arms must need a break."

She shifts her weight, and Mathew willingly goes to him.

"Hey, big boy, I brought you a new toy." He hands Matthew a plastic tractor, then turns back to her. "You seem deep in thought. Care to share?"

"I was just thinking."

He grins. "Does that include me?"

"Stan, it's your engagement party. We can't talk here."

"Tell me that you choose me, and we'll leave right now—tonight."

"I can't do that with Ella and Will flying in. It would ruin the evening. The family hasn't been together for a happy event in over a year. Let's just enjoy the evening."

"Your choice." He shakes his head, and his eyes show disappointment. Then, he walks back to Marie and extends a similar kiss to the one he gave Gabby.

Jealousy rises in Gabby's chest, making it hard to take a deep breath.

Seconds later, Ella is by her side, handing her a glass of chardonnay. "When did you sneak in?"

"Just a minute ago. Did I miss anything?"

"Only Marie sharing her wedding plans. I look awful in pink. I hope she changes her mind. I know you'll be happy with it since pink is your fav."

"I thought the wedding would be small and casual. Am I in the wedding party?" Gabby puts her hand on her chest.

"Of course, silly, and it doesn't sound small to me. Rita and Marie have grand plans." She holds up her glass. "Let's toast to us. It's been too long, Gabby. I've missed you." They clink their glasses.

"Ella, you have no idea how much I've missed our chats. Can you sneak out tonight for some girl time on the porch? Remember when we nabbed that expensive bottle of red from Daddy's cellar the night of the hoedown? We were up until after 2:00 a.m."

"Wow, that was like five years ago. We were young and naïve. No responsibilities. That was the night Richard stormed off because you took up with Brett."

"That seems like ages ago. So much has changed." She lowers her eyes.

"Hey, I'm sorry to bring up bad memories. But thinking ahead to good times, we have a wedding this spring, and bigger than that, Richard will be governor, and you, girlfriend, will be in the mansion living the big life. I'm so proud of you. Sneak another bottle and hide it in Matthew's stroller. Later tonight, I'll walk to your house so as not to disturb the tribe at Stan's place. Deal?"

Gabby bites her lip.

"I've seen that look before. I'll get away, and we'll talk later. Promise." Ella hugs her shoulders. "Let's celebrate with Stan and Marie." Ella pulls her toward the couple.

Before they cross the room, Rita clinks a glass, and King is by her side. "Time to toast! We need a speech from the bride and the groom-to-be."

Just as the words land on their ears, a deafening sound overhead breaks the moment. It gets louder still.

"That sounds like a helicopter," King says. "I believe it's landing."

The family follows King out the front door as a helicopter's landing skids make contact with the ground. The chopper's door opens, and two men immerge.

King runs toward them, hugs the first, and shakes hands with the second. Whoever these men are, King knows them. As they get closer, Gabby's mouth drops open. Richard acknowledges Stan and Marie before hugging Gabby. Incredible! Since when did Richard place family before work?

The second man takes off the baseball cap that hides his face. Brett's face appears out of the evening shadows…Brandon Matthews.

She knew this night would be memorable, but nothing like this ever crossed her mind.

After being welcomed and introduced to the clan, Brandon eventually makes his way toward Gabby and Richard.

"I think we surprised them." He pats Richard on the back.

"That we did. Wonderful idea."

She looks into the faces of both men. "Whose idea was it to drop in?"

Richard speaks first. "I wish it were mine, but it was Brandon's. When I told him that you had to be here for the engagement party and that I was missing a family gathering, he said he could fix it. Guess he did."

"Wow, did he ever."

"You're happy to see me, right?" He plants a kiss on her cheek. "I promised Brandon a home-cooked meal, and he was motivated. Rented us a whirlybird. Super cool. We left the press behind."

Brandon smiles and rolls his eyes.

"Where's Amanda?" Gabby asks.

"Right, I forgot. Show Brandon around while I give her a call. She's probably going crazy not knowing where I am."

"You ditched her?"

He holds her a little tighter, and his wide grin seems as though he's genuinely happy that he's there. "For you, for this...yes." He points to Brandon. "Gabby, get this man The Cowboy. I told him it's the best bourbon in the world. I'll be along soon. I'll promise Amanda that we'll be back before tomorrow's race."

Brandon nods. "Assure her that we'll be back tonight." He scans the horizon. "It's too bad that we race tomorrow. This place is amazing. It would be easy to stay, but then I would be out of a job."

Jamie serves dinner buffet style with the additional unexpected guests. The menu includes smoked beef short ribs and brisket served with a variety of sides. Loud talk drowns the country music playing from the overhead speakers. Lola and Brandon fit right into the group since the King family never knew a stranger.

After dinner, Gabby approaches Brandon, checking out the bookcases in the great room. Turning toward her, he holds a picture frame in his hand.

"That's our wedding photo," she offers.

"You made a lovely couple."

"We were very happy for the short time we were given. I would do almost anything to have him back." Her voice trails off.

"You were beautiful. Still are." His smile is a likeness to Brett, except for the absence of a dimple. "I'm sorry I never got to meet him. Tell me, are we alike? Yes, we look alike, but do we act the same?" He searches for feedback. "If I'm being too forward, I apologize."

She closes her eyes, turning back the hands of time before speaking. "No, it's okay. You should know. Yes, you are very much alike."

"How so?"

"The same mannerisms, like facial expressions. You both hum to music."

His eyes open wide in surprise.

"When we danced at the dedication." She blushes.

"That's right. We did dance." He cocks his head to the side, grinning. "Was I humming? I wasn't aware."

She nods, and her heart flutters as she takes the photo from his hand to replace it on the bookshelf. More talk like this will cause her to get teary-eyed.

"Matthew's a great little guy. He doesn't seem to favor his dad. I guess he looks more like the King side of the family."

The remark hits her at her core. She stays strong and plays it cool. "I'm glad he got to meet his uncle."

"Yes, that does make me an uncle." He sips his bourbon. "Fascinating. Months ago, when my mother was on her deathbed, I felt alone in this world. After she told me I had family, I made it my mission to find you. I hope barging in like this is okay. I'm not insensitive to your feelings. I do care." His stare resembles Brett's so much that her heart skips a beat. He touches her arm, and the warmth travels through her veins. "Tonight has been like a dream come true. Thank you for making me feel welcome, like I am part of your family. It must be grand to be surrounded by so many who love you."

Her eyes tear up, and she's certain that he notices. Her voice trembles. "I must go." After taking two steps and gaining composure, she turns and says, "He would have liked you."

His eyes follow her steps, and he rattles the ice cubes in his glass before ingesting a healthy swallow of bourbon. He's a newcomer, just getting introduced to the dynamics of the King family. However, as he tries to align the facts with his perceptions, something is amiss. It's obvious the widow is still grieving. Disguising her grief behind her smile seems to go unnoticed by those she holds close. She's a good actress, but her skills break down with him. How can she and Richard be engaged while her grief is still evident? These past few weeks, he's also witnessed the fire between Richard and Amanda. Does he have a responsibility to his twin brother to protect Gabby, or should he mind his own business? He rubs his chin.

Later in the evening, along with a bit of fanfare, Jamie announces the serving of dessert. Rita emerges from the kitchen, holding a three-tiered cake, a replica of a wedding cake, and places it before the newly engaged couple.

"Cut this. You should practice for your big day." She winks before handing a silver knife to her son. "Read it. I had it engraved. It's your first present as a couple." She claps her hands together, then glances in Gabby's direction.

Stan holds the knife up to the light. "Wow. It says Mr. and Mrs. Stanley Adams."

"That's so special and very thoughtful," Marie says. "Thank you." She reaches up on tiptoes to kiss Stan.

Gabby pays close attention to the interaction, watching Marie's body language for clues. The couple giggles and touches one another as they perform the ritual of cutting a wedge and then giving each other bites where the sweet lands more on their faces than their mouths. No one would be the wiser of the undertones that their relationship is less than ideal.

Lola bounces Matthew on her lap and converses with Ella, who holds Gracie. Gabby's unsure if Lola remembers her assignment to evaluate Marie's behavior. However, it's obvious that the newly engaged couple is happy.

Richard stands with his arm around her, giving the impression that their relationship shows equal stability. As he pulls her in close, she gets a whiff of a spicy fragrance and bites the inside of her cheek. The telltale clue supports Amanda's claim to Richard. She twirls her sapphire and diamond ring, remembering Richard's words when she accepted it. Maybe her relationship is just like the royals when Diana discovered Camilla's hold on Prince Charles. She lowers her head.

"This will be us next year. We'll pick a date after the election." He squeezes her shoulders. "Our wedding will be a grand affair. I hope you're up for it. I want all of Texas, if not the entire United States, watching. Stan and Marie think theirs will be special, but nothing will compare to our big day."

Before she has time to analyze his words, Brandon approaches and looks at his phone as he addresses Richard. "I hate to take you away from this lovely lady, but we need to head back. I called Hank to start up the chopper."

"You heard the man. I'm out of here." He leaves her side to say his farewells to Rita and King.

Gabby rubs the back of her neck, hoping that with the crowd and the celebration, she is the only one who notices that Richard hasn't spent a second with his son. Even Brandon got down on the floor and played with Matthew. Matthew needs a father for a strong male role model. Who best fills the void if Richard doesn't own up to his responsibility? She always dreamed that her son would grow up on the ranch and cherish the legacy her grandparents created. She doesn't want him in the limelight with every move he makes drawing praise or criticism.

Lola waves her hand in front of her. "Gabby, what I would give to get a glimpse of your thoughts. You're like a million miles away."

"Oh, sorry. Where's Matthew? We should be going as well. It's past his bedtime."

"There." Lola points to Stan holding Matthew, pushing his new tractor as it plows through a pretend field on the couch. "He's so good with him. He'll make a great father someday."

She fakes a smile. "I'll see Richard off." She runs out the front door as Richard and Brandon board the helicopter. Richard turns, waving at King and Rita. Gabby calls his name, but he must not have heard her over the engine's roar. Brandon acknowledges her with a wave and blows her a kiss. Within a second, the helicopter leaves the ground, and the wind generated lashes her hair, stinging her face.

CHAPTER 22

The next morning, Gabby wakes early, quietly enters her son's room, and gently kisses his cheek. After last evening's surprise visit from Richard and Brandon, she'll follow suit with her own surprise. It's a push since she slept only a few hours. She and Ella had their long-overdue girlfriend chat after the engagement party, and it lasted past midnight. Her change in plans results from their discussion.

During their college days, Gabby was frequently the advice-giver; now, the roles appear to have reversed. Ella readily surmised that if Gabby wanted clarity in her relationship with Richard and with his position as governor, it required an investment of effort, energy, and, most importantly, time. Ella's logic implied that instead of distancing herself, Gabby should jump into deep waters and completely immerse herself in the political scene with Richard. The results will prove infallible; she will either sink or swim.

Ella made it seem simple—a basic cause-and-effect theory. But Gabby wasn't totally honest with Ella since she never disclosed the side of the equation involving Stan's confession of love. No need to further complicate an already complex situation. Heeding Ella's advice, she'll drive back to the city to attend the F1 race, which requires her to hit the road before the sun peeks above the horizon.

Before these plans were put into words, Jamie had already consented to babysit Matthew, allowing Lola the freedom to get the scoop first-hand about equine and hippotherapy for her midterm assignment. Together, Marie and Stan promised both an interview and a personal experience by treating Lola as if she is a client needing therapy. With everyone busy attending to their own agendas and Matthew's care arranged, no one will notice that she's gone.

She'll put 100 percent of her efforts into Richard's political life for the days remaining before the election. Since her relationship with Richard is tenuous, will this unite them? If the answer is yes, will holding the position of First Lady of Texas be fulfilling? And if after giving the campaign her best and her relationship with Richard shows no improvement is she willing to sacrifice her personal life to make improvements in the lives of the citizens of Texas? She needs answers.

CHAPTER 23

After a relaxing drive allowing her to sing along with the radio, Gabby arrives at campaign headquarters and unlocks the door. The headquarters is closed on Sunday mornings, but the lights are on today. A few minutes ago, she called Richard. When he didn't pick up, she left a voice message, "You're not the only one who has surprises. I'm here for the race. Pick me up. If you're already on your way, I'll take an Uber. Call me back."

An easy explanation for the lights would be that someone had forgotten, but now she hears a pounding, alerting her to investigate. Reluctantly, she quietly steps toward Richard's office. She grabs an umbrella on her way, thinking it could be useful. She never wishes to strike anyone, but holding it makes her feel safer. She read that the city suffers from an increase in crime. However, the noise could be from rats who managed to crawl into the boxes of swag, surviving the transatlantic passage on a cargo ship. It wouldn't be the first time. The banging occurs again. She shudders, envisioning the size of an animal that can make such a noise. Her knuckles are white as her grip tightens.

Slowly, she enters Richard's dark office. The door is open, so she reaches for the light switch. The sight before her is unsettling, but she's determined to remain poised. "Should I have knocked?" Her voice is even and steady in contrast to her flip-flopping stomach.

The pair before her separate, adjusting their clothing.

"Gabby, what are you doing here?" Richard's voice is sharp and commanding, as if she's a child being scolded by a parent. He quickly steps away from Amanda, then walks around his desk. He clears his throat. "Amanda was just fixing my tie. She makes a neater knot."

"I'm sure she does. Her skills are impeccable..." Gabby stands tall with her hands on her hips and shifts her eyes to Amanda, who is wearing a Cheshire-cat-style grin as she buttons her dress.

"Amanda, could you give us a minute? Thanks, sweetie." Gabby is pleased with her sarcastic tone and plants a fake smile, motioning toward the door with the tip of her umbrella. Seconds ago, she was hesitant about what to do with the feeble stick; now, she suppresses the overwhelming urge to swat Amanda. The young campaign manager pushes past her, and Gabby notices the exaggerated swagger in her gait. Instead of being embarrassed at getting caught in a compromising act, it's as though she's flaunting the incident, her actions saying to the fiancé, "I warned you."

"What was that? Work, I presume?" Gabby slowly walks toward him.

He looks at her with blank eyes and shrugs his shoulders. "If I recall, I invited you, and you were busy doing whatever it is that you do." His eyes lower to his desk, and he shuffles some papers. "Don't make it a big deal. We're adults here. You know that Amanda and I have a history."

"I believe the proper tense would be past: you *had* a history. Yes, we are adults. Adults that made promises to each other. You told me it was over. Your exact words when you slipped this ring on my finger were that you had changed, and we were in this race together. You and *me*."

She throws up her hands.

"You're not around. If you want to find fault, look in the mirror." His stare is glaring.

She stands with closed eyes, then shakes her head, at a loss for words. *How dare he place the blame on me.*

He chuckles. "You're so naïve."

She regains composure. "Naïve, yes, because I believe in loyalty, trust, and exclusivity. Let's put this to the test…what would the citizens of Texas say? Maybe it's time I give an interview, paraphrasing the words of the Princess of Wales in her best British accent, "There are three of us in this relationship, so it's a bit crowded." Perhaps I'll chat with Daddy—make him aware of the disgusting scum you continue to be."

"Your daddy will say, 'Princess, it's time to grow up.' Gabby, you believe in the fairy tale—the happily-ever-after. Life doesn't work that way. Don't do anything stupid." He shakes his head, then displays a touch of remorse. "Gabby, our goal is around the corner—the election is a week away. We're close to living the life we've always dreamed of. I'll make it up to you. Promise."

She has seen this look before, the one resembling a lost puppy dog. "And how are you going to do that?"

"After the election, we can go away, start fresh. Pick anywhere,

anywhere in the world." He stares into her unforgiving eyes. "Think of your daddy, Gabby. He wants this. He wants this for you, for me, for all of us. Don't ruin it."

Does he think the lure of a lavish holiday will atone for this indiscretion?

"And Amanda?"

"Forget about her."

"You make it sound so easy. Forget about her? Did Princess Diana forget about Camilla? History shows that Charles never forgot Camilla." She places her hands on her hips. "You embarrass yourself with your whore hanging on you. With your arrogance, you act as though you've already won the election. You're getting sloppy. That's not only my opinion. Do you read any of those?" She points to the magazines and newspapers on his desk. "Surely, Amanda has alerted you about your recent drop in the polls." She throws her long blond hair behind her shoulder. "And you're worrying about me ruining everything; look at yourself. What is your plan?"

She takes a few more steps, narrowing the gap between them. As she nears, her nostrils detect the same spicy fragrance she remembers smelling when they stood on the steps of the governor's mansion. And the same perfume last night. She would like to deck him and toss her engagement ring like a scorned lover in a movie scene. She steps closer, now only inches from his face.

"Amanda isn't as skilled as you think." She smiles, then carefully reaches out to readjust his tie. Her stare is cold. Then, using the tie like a noose, she grips it with a force so great that it jerks his head forward. With his face an inch from hers, she strikes like a viper and bites his upper lip.

The blow comes as a surprise to the unsuspecting victim.

"Ouch, what did you do that for?" He holds his hand up to his mouth. "I have an interview. Damn." He turns to look in the mirror hanging on the wall behind his desk. "God, Gabby, it's bleeding."

"You're lucky. You could be sporting a black eye or worse." She swipes her hand across his desk, scattering folders and magazines over the floor. The taste of revenge is sweet.

"When you're finished acting like a child, pick those up." He pulls his shoulders back, waving his finger. "Grow up, Gabby. You barge in here unannounced…"

She abruptly turns and exits. She calls over her shoulder. "Call your bitch to pick it up."

He screams after her. "You're crazy…insane." He continues to dab at his lip, checking the blood on his finger.

She strides into the main room, takes a seat, crosses her legs, and picks up a booklet from the coffee table. Oblivious to Amanda's stare, Gabby flips the brochure over.

"Richard had an accident, and he may need your help." Her outward demeanor hides her inner rage. It's surprising that she's able to remain calm. "And after you clean up his mess, you're free for the remainder of the day. Your services won't be needed at the race." She places the pamphlet down and views the young woman with pity. "Richard can be, let's just say…difficult. You deserve a break after everything he puts you through and what he does to you." She raises her eyebrows. "This next week will be intense. Go rest and recharge. You look like you could use a bit of refreshing. We can't have the public see you all a mess."

Richard and Gabby's limo drives through the VIP gate at the race-track. Silence prevailed between them during the thirty-minute ride. It seems to be a standoff, with each weighing the importance of public opinion at this critical time. If Gabby runs to King, she's certain of his advice: the election overrides any personal woes—suck it up and save it until after the votes are counted. For her daddy, she'll play it cool and not make a scene. For now, she'll keep this to herself. Gabby uses this time to call Lola to inquire about her day at the equine center, and then she calls Jamie to check on Matthew.

Her face is calm, as if the incident at headquarters was in the distant past. She's an expert at faking emotions, especially when it comes to Richard. She recalls Brandon's observation of Richard's relationship with Amanda: "They seem close." Was this a tactful warning from a family member, alerting her that he saw something very intimate between them? Even so, this incident at campaign headquarters isn't a surprise and, to her best guess, not a one-time endeavor.

She turns and leans forward to check his lip and notes that it remains swollen, but the bleeding has stopped. She's not sorry for her initial fury because he has hurt her with deeper emotional blows over the years of their intermittent relationship.

She wonders if Richard's long face signals disappointment about the damage to their relationship, or is he pouting because he would rather Amanda be by his side? *Poor Richard. His behavior is like that of a spoiled child.* This thought puts a smile on her face.

Shortly after stopping at their destination, the chauffeur opens the passenger door. As they exit the limousine, Richard tries to hold her hand, but she pushes past him, leaving him a few paces behind as she interacts with the crowd. She's aware that she's purposely breaking the standard. According to the rules, the candidate always leads. *To hell with the rules.*

Even with a security escort, it takes the couple thirty minutes to shake hands and engage with the crowd, encouraging them to vote on election day. Once in the owner's suite located inside the F1 Paddock Club, Steven Prime enthusiastically greets them and introduces them to several of his honored guests. Gabby recognizes a few faces from other social events, and several unfamiliar guests make references to being close friends with King. She nods her head as if she has met them in the past.

As the start of the F1 race gets closer, the crowd in the stands and those in the owner's suite get louder. It's nearly impossible to talk to the person sitting next to her. Richard is engaged in conversation in the front row while she sits in the back and wonders how Brandon is managing. He and the team have worked months preparing for today. Silently, she wishes him good luck and knows that Brett would have loved to have met his brother.

CHAPTER 24

The King Ranch

The helicopter circles before landing at the King property near the ranch house. Rusty is giving directions using hand signals. When it lands, two medics carrying black medical bags follow him into the house.

"Who called them? Damn it." King's voice is harsh.

"I did. Wayne, calm yourself," Rita yells. "It's your heart. It's not like you have a stomachache."

King moves to get up from the sofa. The paramedics pull equipment from their bags.

"Please be still while I get your vitals." The paramedic activates the blood pressure cuff and places the pulse oximeter on his finger.

"You're making a fuss over nothing. I'm fine."

Rita stands with her arms crossed. "If you're fine…great. I'll believe it when I hear that from them.

The second paramedic places a nasal cannula in King's nose. "Rate your pain from one to ten, with ten being the greatest."

"Pain, my pain's gone, and I don't need any oxygen. Don't you have sicker patients to worry about?" He pulls the nasal prongs from his nostrils, then gestures to the medics to shoo them away.

"That would be you right now, Mr. King. We're going to put these electrodes on to get an EKG. I'm going to lift your shirt. Please hold still."

"That's unnecessary. I told you I'm fine."

Rita's hands move to her hips as she hovers near the couch. "I'm sorry this stubborn old coot is being disrespectful."

"Don't go apologizing for me," King barks.

"Sir, please lie back and be still. Just a few seconds more." After the EKG strip passes from the hands of one paramedic to the other, they nod in agreement.

"Mr. King, we're taking you for a ride. Mac, fetch the stretcher." The second paramedic gets off his knees and walks out the door.

King pulls his shirt over his belly and sits up straight. "Stretcher, I don't need a stretcher. I have two perfectly good legs."

"Mr. King, this is serious. With the ST elevation on your EKG, you need further evaluation. You may be having a heart attack. We need to move quickly to get you to the hospital."

"Wayne," Rita gasps, then places her hands over her mouth. There is fear in her eyes as she turns to the paramedic. "A heart attack, are you sure?"

"The blood work will confirm, but from what we're seeing on the EKG, it's most likely."

Rita rushes to King's side. Rusty places his arm around his wife, whose eyes fill with tears as they fear for the man who has given them a family.

"Tell me it isn't so," Jamie says, her voice a whisper.

King grimaces and holds his left arm. "The pain's coming back." His breaths are rapid and shallow.

The paramedic reapplies the nasal cannula and increases the oxygen flow before starting an intravenous drip. King no longer protests.

Before the second paramedic returns from the Medivac with the stretcher, a second intravenous line infuses a dextrose solution into King's arm. After the doctors reviewed the electrocardiogram sent via Bluetooth, they decided to skip the smaller local hospital and transport King straight to the regional trauma facility that specializes in the latest research and cardiology services.

Hearing this side of the conversation, Rita grabs her phone and purse. "I'm going with you." She then leans close to her husband. "Don't you consider for one second leaving me, you ole goat."

"You'd miss me?" His eyes smile, and he cups her face with an extended hand.

"Put it this way, if you leave me, I'll kill you myself." She pokes him in the arm.

He grabs her finger. "Glad you care, but I'm not going anywhere. The election is next week."

"That damn election. All this stress. It's too much. I've been telling you to back off. Look what it's doing to you." Her brow is crossed.

"Hey, I'm gonna be fine, promise."

"I'm holding you to that." She squeezes his hand. "I love you."

"I love you, too." He pats her hand. "You worry too much."

"Mr. King, time to go. Let's get you in the air and on your way."

The paramedics pick up the stretcher and head out the door with Rita trailing close behind.

Wayne's face is pale, and the mighty king of the oil and cattle ranchers looks old and frail. He turns to study Rusty and Jamie, who follow along and nod as if saying good-bye.

Rusty's eyes fill with water, and he blinks back a tear, watching his longtime friend disappear into the helicopter's cabin.

Rita yells over the roar of the helicopter's engine and rotor blades. "I'll call as soon as we land. I'll let Gabby know."

Forty-five minutes later, the medical helicopter lands on the roof of the regional trauma center. King's stretcher wheels through the double doors as Rita rushes to keep up. A receptionist motions to get her attention, guiding her into the small registration office. As she is filling out the initial document, she jumps as overhead speakers bellow four beeps followed by "Code Blue Coronary Care, Code Blue Coronary Care."

As they repeat the sequence, the hairs on her arms rise. "Is that Wayne? I need to go." Her eyes are wide and full of fear.

"Mrs. King," the receptionist says, "the best way to help your husband is to complete the admission process. Please, sit down. I don't know if the code is for your husband or another patient. Even so, you won't be allowed in the room. Our doctors and nurses are exceptional. He's in good hands."

"What if he needs me? I should be there."

"Dr. White will find you right here in this waiting room when Mr. King is ready to receive visitors. I know this is difficult, but these forms are necessary so your husband can get the best care possible. Is he allergic to any medications?"

"No, none that I'm aware of. Are you sure they'll find me?" Rita looks from side to side.

"I'm positive. It's the first place they'll look. Now, let's continue. Do you have a list of your husband's current meds?"

After completing the forms, Rita paces the waiting room, banging her fist into her left palm, attempting to relieve her anxious tension. Jamie had answered her phone calls, but her call to Gabby immediately went to voice mail. She's aware the F1 race runs this afternoon since Gabby drove early this morning to stand by Richard's side. Understandably, Gabby hasn't returned her call; it's probably for the best because she'll ask questions, and at present, the answers are few and incomplete. There is nothing Gabby's presence can do to help her daddy.

After rummaging through her purse to retrieve a Kleenex, the hospital chaplain is by Rita's side.

"Mrs. King. I'm Pastor Jason." He's much younger than she envisioned for someone responsible for guiding sick patients to God. He's a generation younger than her sons. He doesn't wear a clerical collar, so he could easily be mistaken for another visitor. "I came to see if you need anything." His eyes speak kindness. "Times like these are tough on family members. You feel helpless."

She uses Kleenex to wipe her nose. "When can I see him?"

"Soon...he told me to tell you to stop worrying...and that he loves you." Pastor Jason reaches out to hold her hand.

Her face lightens. "You saw Wayne? How?"

"I get called to every Code."

Her brief ray of hope disappears, and she gasps, realizing that the earlier announcement was for her husband. She runs her fingers through her hair and leans into the clergyman, sobbing.

He pats her shoulder. "Do you have any family members I can call…someone to wait here with you?"

She sniffles. "I made a few calls. His daughter has yet to call me back, although there's really nothing anyone can do. I wish I could see Wayne or at least talk with the doctor. I would feel better knowing what's happening."

"I assure you that this hospital has great doctors and that your husband is getting the best care possible. I'll wait here with you. Would it be okay if we prayed?"

With tear-stained cheeks, she looks up at the young pastor before bowing her head to join him in prayer.

Still deep in these thoughts and prayers, she misses Dr. White's initial entrance. After closing with an *amen*, Pastor Jason hands her his card, instructing her to call him any time, and then leaves.

She turns to observe Dr. White standing quietly, checking his phone. He's dressed in blue scrubs with a matching cap. She watches as he removes his face mask. He puts his phone in his pocket, then picks at his nails as though delaying their conversation. A lump forms in her throat, and she makes the sign of the cross, anticipating bad news.

"Dr. White?" Her voice trembles.

"Oh, Mrs. King, sorry." He clears his throat. "Mr. King gave us a bit of a scare, but we got him fixed as well as we could, and he's in recovery. The nurses are getting ready to transfer him to the coronary care unit. Your husband had a heart attack. Fortunately, he came here in the early stage. He had the care he needed when his heart stopped…"

Her eyes open wide. "Oh my, his heart stopped?"

"Yes. We were able to revive him and immediately took him to the heart catheterization lab and performed a successful angioplasty. That's a procedure where we thread a catheter up through his groin into his heart. At the end of the catheter is a balloon, which we can inflate to open the coronary artery walls and restore blood flow. Because of the quick timing of the procedure to the start of the occlusion, the initial insult was lessened. We put in a stent."

"Does that mean that he'll be okay?"

The doctor smiles. "He may be better than he was before. He needs to rest his heart for a few weeks. Do me a favor and remind him. He seems anxious to get out of here. I know the type."

"That's my Wayne. He's always on the go. I'll sit on him if it comes down to that." She clasps her hands together. "I can't thank you enough for everything you and the staff have done. I thought I lost him."

"The credit goes to you. He's doing well because you were proactive and got him here. He told me he didn't think it was anything and wasn't too keen on coming in. Many people wait, and then more damage is done—sometimes, it's irreversible. He's one of the lucky ones." His phone beeps.

"They're looking for me. Do you have any questions?"

She shakes her head. "When can I see him?"

"The nurse will come when he's settled in the unit. It should be in the next few minutes. I'll be here all day, so if you have any questions, have them call me."

As he opens the door to leave, Gabby rushes into the waiting room. Her hair is disheveled, and she's short of breath.

"I got here as soon as I could."

Gabby first notices Rita's dried tears and gives her a hug. "I'm so sorry I didn't get your message sooner. The receptionist says that Daddy is in the coronary care unit."

Rita nods. "He had a heart attack, but the doctor says he's going to be as good as new. God has been good to us."

Gabby bites her lip. "How…when…"

Rita starts to answer but halts as the nurse enters. "Anyone here in the King family?"

Rita waves. "Yes, that's us."

Then Rita places her arm through Gabby's. "Let's see Wayne and find out how he's doing for ourselves."

"There's a sight that makes this old heart skip a beat. Two beautiful women by my bed. I must have died and gone to heaven." He chuckles.

"Wayne, that's nothing to joke about." Rita takes his hand and leans in for a kiss.

"I'm not joking. There are two beautiful women…"

Rita pushes her two fingers against his lips to quiet him.

Gabby takes a place at the bedside next to Rita. She thinks her daddy looks pale. An IV drips fluid through tubing taped to his arm, and there's a green oxygen cannula in his nose. He's flat on his back, making him appear weak, and there's a large sandbag on his groin. It may have been the large circle of blood on the sheet that tipped the scales toward the reality of his situation. Even though she is trying her best to keep her emotions in tow, a tear manages to escape and wander down her cheek. She turns to wipe it away, but she gets caught.

Her daddy's expression changes from making light of his situation to showing that he shares her concern.

He shakes his head. "Aww, princess, I'm so sorry."

The hospital atmosphere has a domino effect; in seconds, all three are sobbing. Rita, crying, leans her head into King's shoulder. He pats her back to help ease the pain.

Gabby stands and looks up to the ceiling, using both hands to wipe her eyes. "You have nothing, absolutely nothing, to be sorry about." She takes in a deep breath to compose herself. "I'm so thankful that you're alive. I still need you, Daddy." She bites her lower lip, and he motions for her to approach from the other side of the bed. When she does, he wraps his big arm around her and kisses her cheek. The three hang together quietly.

"I told you I was a lucky man—holding two beautiful women, *my* beautiful women."

"What's going on in here? A group hug? I want in." Stan stands at the doorway and then rushes to his mother's side.

"Stan, I'm glad you're here." Rita squeezes his hand.

Stan nods to Gabby. "I came as soon as I heard. Everyone is here—Rusty, Jamie, Will, and Ella. They won't let us all come back. If we take turns, everyone will get a short visit before the nurses kick us out."

King's eyes light up. "Thanks, it means a lot to me. Gabby, send Rusty and Jamie in next."

"Of course, Daddy." Gabby folds her hands together and studies Stan's face as she backs out of the room.

As Gabby enters the waiting room, Matthew reaches out to her as she lifts him from Rusty's arms. Her eyes follow the elder couple, dear friends to her daddy, as they walk through the double metal doors leading to the CCU (Coronary Care Unit). Jamie and Rusty are as close as family, and she adores them. Gabby squeezes her son, rocking him back and forth. This close call with King has opened her sentimental side like an old wound. It brings to her mind that there is nothing more precious than family—her daddy is her family, Jamie and Rusty are her family, Will and Ella are her family, Stan is her family, and her son is her family. Brandon wants to be family. But what does that make Richard? It upends her like a rug pulled out from under her feet. She doesn't consider him family.

In the waiting room, Will is pacing in front of the windows at the far side of the room, and Ella holds a sleeping Gracie on her lap.

Gabby sits next to her best friend. "I'm so glad you're here." She squeezes Ella's hand.

"Will's on the phone getting our flights rebooked. We were going to leave this afternoon. But how could we?" Ella continues to bring her up to speed on the events leading to King's hospitalization.

When Stan returns from the unit, Gabby stands. "He's still doing okay?" She bounces Matthew on her hip.

"Yep, Jamie and Rusty will be coming out, so Will and Ella can go next. How are you holding up?"

"Not too well. This whole thing caught me by surprise. I didn't know that Daddy had heart issues. Ella's been filling me in. Daddy can be stubborn." She rubs Matthew's back. "Today has not been a good day."

"More than what happened to your dad? Care to share?"

"It seems trivial in comparison to what Daddy is going through." She searches for more faces. "Where's Marie and Lola?"

"Since Lola's paper is due in a few weeks, she wants to research a minimum of two equine techniques and two hippotherapy techniques.

We still had one technique to show when the call came through. We agreed I should go, give them updates, and they can meet here later. Lola needs to return for her classes tomorrow." He looks for her acknowledgment; instead, she stares off as if in another world. "Gabby, is that good by you…if Lola comes back later?"

"What? Oh, sure." She shakes her head, trying to blink away the tears.

"Gabby…"

She finds comfort mixed with compassion and concern in his kind eyes. She falls into his arms, sobbing. "This all has been too much. This morning was upsetting, and now with Daddy's health spiraling…it's overwhelming."

As Stan holds her and rocks her back and forth, the outer world vanishes. Gabby is in crisis, and like so many times in the past, he's here, holding her steady. He hopes she feels their connection, one he's known all along. He prays for something, anything, to convince her they should be together. But his hope rides a timeline. As the days on the calendar flip quickly over to tomorrow, his promise to move forward with Marie gets nearer. He made that promise and sealed it on a star. At times like this, he regrets the decision of his second wish.

He buries his face in her hair, breathing in the delicate floral scent. Can't she feel how their bodies melt perfectly into each other? In this moment, holding his true love close, his spirit strengthens. A spirit previously worn thin like a fragile garment whose threads are ready to give way feels stronger as if mending. Can the creator of the universe

189

grant him his dream? At this precious moment with her in his arms, he's already dreading the emptiness he'll feel when it ends.

Ella studies the scene unfolding between her brother-in-law and her best friend. Anyone would be blind if they missed the obvious affection between the two. Last night, during their girl chat on the porch, Gabby shared her indecision about Richard and life as the governor's wife, never mentioning Stan. She has seen with her own eyes that since Stan met Gabby five years ago, he has worn his feelings for her on his sleeve. This has always been one-sided. However, this embrace causes her to suspect that there's more to Gabby's indecision than what she disclosed. Amanda's name was mentioned several times in their late-night girl talk. Perhaps Stan's name should have graced their conversation as well.

Ella is confused. At Stan and Marie's engagement party, they seemed the perfect example of a loving couple embarking on the next big step in their relationship. Today is not the day to confront Gabby about her love life, but the two women need another serious heart-to-heart, and soon.

Matthew squirms in Gabby's arms, so she pushes away and wipes her eyes. "I'm sorry. I'm sorry I broke down like that."

He stands and puts his hands in his back pockets. "No, it's fine. Really."

She lowers her eyes to avert the sudden awkwardness. "You're always there when I need you. Thanks again."

"I thought Richard would be with you."

"Richard is at the race. I came from there when I saw the call. I never told him. I left as quickly as I could." She rubs her forehead. "I have a nasty headache. It could be stress or from not eating. Somehow, I missed breakfast and lunch. I'll see if Matthew has some Cheerios in his bag."

"Here, let me hold the little guy." Stan holds out his arms, but Matthew leans his head closer to his mother. "Okay, you stay with your mama, and I'll check the bag for Cheerios." After rummaging through the diaper bag, he hands a plastic container to Gabby. "There's a cafeteria. I'll get us some sandwiches and coffee. It could prove to be a long wait."

"Stan?"

"Yes?"

"Thanks. When this is over, we need to talk."

He nods in agreement and offers a tight smile before turning away.

CHAPTER 25

In the City

It was dark outside as Gabby entered her downtown condo. She had invited Rita to spend the night, but Rita refused to leave the hospital. Gabby would have done the same, but she has Matthew to consider, so she left after evening visiting hours ended. She's holding Rita to her promise to call if King's condition changes. Besides, Will, Ella, and Gracie were with him before leaving to stay at a hotel near the airport. Their flight leaves midafternoon, so they can visit King before flying back to Washington, and Will can get back to the accounting firm.

After putting her son to bed, Gabby turns on the television. From the scene of champagne being opened and sprayed on a team in red and gold uniforms, Gabby understands that the Mercedes team did not win the prized trophy. Although they had placed first in the qualifying round, their team took second place. She'll text Brandon and congratulate him on the team's second-place finish.

After checking her phone for a missed call or previous text, she realizes there has been no word from Richard. He's probably upset she left without giving him notice, and he still may not know that her daddy almost died today. He deserves insight about her daddy, even though she believes Richard is worse than pond scum.

She punches his number into her cell. "Richard, it's me."

"Where in the hell did you go? You shouldn't have dismissed Amanda if you weren't going to stay."

"Richard…"

"Don't *Richard* me. You can't go embarrassing me like that in public. I…we have an image to uphold. You're never going to get it, are you? This is not about you. I know it's hard for you to hear, but this is bigger than you. Okay, this is bigger than our future. This is about the future of Texas." He pauses to catch his breath. "What's wrong with you? You attack me. You embarrass me."

"D-d-d-daddy had a heart attack. His heart stopped, Richard. He almost died." Her voice trembles with fear drenched in anger. "No one dared to trouble you at the racetrack. No one dared to pull you away from shaking hands and getting votes." She takes a deep breath. "I went to the hospital to be by his side. He's my daddy. You wouldn't be where you are without him." She closes her eyes and sobs.

"Oh, Gabby. I'm sorry. I didn't know." There is a beat of silence. Then, "Is he okay?"

The phone falls from her trembling hands.

"Gabby, Gabby, Gabby…hey, I'm sorry. I didn't know. Talk to me. Tell me all the facts."

She picks up the phone and hears a familiar woman's voice in the background.

"You're with Amanda? Exactly where are you?"

"We're at the Driscoll."

"At the hotel?"

"It's not like we got a room. We're having dinner."

She looks at her watch. "This late?"

"We're finishing."

"It's ten o'clock. You don't call. You don't make any effort to stop and think that maybe, just maybe, something may have happened. It's not always about you, Richard."

"I was having dinner. It's not a big deal. Geez, can you tell me about your dad?"

"Richard, I must go. I'll tell you about Daddy when you get home, here to my condo. I assume that will be soon." She disconnects.

Twenty minutes later, her doorbell rings. Did Richard forget his key? She turns on the porch light, and Stan waves.

"Hi! Is Daddy all right?" She opens the door to let him in.

"He's doing as well as can be expected. He's asleep. I just left Rita. With a private room, they brought in a cot, and she's spending the night next to his bed. Will and Ella checked into the hotel next to the airport."

"Thank God. I was worried."

"I hope it's not too late."

"No, no, it's fine. Please, come in."

He takes her hands in his. "You're still trembling. Now, I'm concerned."

"It's been a rough day. So, why aren't you with Marie?"

"Marie? Oh, she and Lola are with Brandon and the team—out celebrating. It's not like there is anything they can do at the hospital. Marie and Lola really hit it off. They're almost the same age, so they have things in common." He shakes his head. "With King not completely out of the woods, I can't celebrate...and I'm worried about you." He squeezes her hands. "Hey, talk to me. What's going on?"

"Stan…" She bites her lip. "How about some hot tea? I have some chocolate chip cookies too."

"Now, you're talking. That's a pun." He laughs.

"Follow me." She leads him into the kitchen. "Have a seat." She ushers him toward the breakfast room table, then places a cookie jar in the center before turning to the sink and filling the tea kettle with water to heat on the stove.

Rummaging through her pantry to find different flavors of tea-bags, she says, "It's been one of those days. Daddy's heart attack… thank God he was at the hospital when he went into cardiac arrest. Then, if that's not bad enough, Richard is cheating with Amanda. I caught them together this morning." She turns to face him. "We have mint, berry, and lemon."

"Mint sounds good. Continue."

"He didn't deny it. There's no denying it. I found them together, so I bit him."

"You bit him?"

"Right on the lip. He was bleeding. I was actually happy, happy that I hurt him. I'm turning into a heartless creature. But he deserves it. He's terrible. He never spends time with Matthew. It's his son, for God's sake. He should want to spend time with his son. I shouldn't have to beg him." She puts her hands on her hips. "Right now, I hate him."

The tea kettle whistles. She pours the hot water into the cups and places one cup in front of Stan. He sat up straight when she mentioned the cheating part and remained quiet.

"This heart thing with Daddy. It's too much." She runs her hands through her hair and sits across from Stan.

He stirs his tea. "For what it's worth, the doctors say King is going to be fine. What are you going to do about Richard? What more do you need to convince you to leave him?"

"I'm kind of stuck. I can't leave Richard now."

"How so?"

"One week before the election. I do the Hilary Clinton thing and stand by my man. Although, the thought is rather repulsive. Why doesn't he see that being an attentive father will get him those coveted votes? He promised we would be a family. It's what Daddy wanted."

"Whoa there. I keep coming back to the same question time and time again. What do *you* want? That's the question you should be asking." Stan leans back in his chair.

Her facial muscles tense. "Really, you're asking me that when you're marrying Marie because that's what your mother wants. How is this any different?"

"Is that what you think? I thought I was clear. I love you. I want you. You know that. My feelings haven't changed." He reaches across the table, but she pulls her hand away.

"Rita has made it clear that she wants you with Marie."

"My mother doesn't get to decide."

"But you're so happy together. I can see that. Everyone sees it."

"Gabby, this is crazy. I'm going through the motions. I've always loved you.

However, if things don't change and I'm not your choice, I will marry Marie in the spring. I've put my life on hold long enough."

"I'm such a mess. Maybe you would be better off with her. I have so much baggage." She hangs her head and stirs her tea.

He stands behind her, massaging her shoulders before kissing her on the back of her neck.

"It's just been a bad day. I know that for political aesthetics, King wants Richard and you together. After the election, you can break free. Tonight, am I with Marie? No, I'm here—here with you. Come." He pulls her from the chair and holds her tight. Then his hand guides her chin. Their eyes meet. His lips find her forehead and then travel to her mouth, but she turns away.

She can't do this. It's been weeks since their first kiss on the night of the dedication, and she has relived and fantasized about that one kiss a thousand times. She's been eager for more—one more taste, one more moment. Does she need to feel the magic to evaluate if this can last a lifetime? But with the turmoil of the day, she pushes him away. "Please, don't."

She hears a key in the lock and jerks away to see Richard's large frame coming through the doorway.

"Reporters followed me home. Gabby, pull the curtains." His eyes roam over the teacups on the table. "Stan, thanks for staying with Gabby. I called the hospital, and the charge nurse gave me the latest update. You had just left." He gestures toward Stan. "King's too old and stubborn for a heart attack to do him in."

"Richard," she says, placing her hand over her heart.

He comes to her side and squeezes her shoulder. "I shouldn't make light of the situation. My bad. I could tell from our phone call that you're frazzled." She moves out of his embrace to close the curtain and wonders if the reporters saw her with Stan.

He nods to Stan. "Again, thanks for being with my girl. I had a full schedule, and it's hard to get away this close to the election, even for an emergency. Have a safe drive home."

She cocks her head in protest. "It's too late for Stan to drive home. We can offer him the couch."

"Thanks, not necessary." Stan jingles a set of keys. "Mother offered me their condo."

She sighs in relief. Having Stan and Richard under the same roof would create additional stress. "That's even better. Much nicer than my little place, and you'll have a king-size bed. Give me a report on the steam shower they recently installed. I hear from Rita that it's divine. Call me when you wake up, and we'll go to the hospital together."

She ushers him to the door. "I'll see you in the morning." She looks at him with raised eyebrows and whispers. "That was close."

"I don't care if he saw us," Stan says as he kisses her cheek.

"I care if the reporters saw us. That would make the news."

He shrugs his shoulders and turns his back.

She watches as he gets in his car and drives away.

CHAPTER 26

The next morning, Gabby is quick to grab the newspaper off the front porch. Getting the paper delivered is inexpensive pampering since she enjoys the feel and smell of the newsprint during her leisurely read over morning coffee. She's aware that it's not proper environmentally, but she'll hold on to her vice as long as it's printed and available.

She holds her breath, opening the paper to view the full front page. Her eyes nervously scan the headlines and photos, then she blows out, releasing air from her lungs along with the tension that's been building. The paper has no mention or pictures of her and Stan in their brief moment of passion. *Thank you, God.* Then, she checks social media sites. Finding nothing, she looks up in gratitude. The memory of the fallout from her luncheon meeting with Brandon still burns fresh. The election is eight days away.

Moments later, Richard is in the shower, and Matthew is in his highchair eating oatmeal and applesauce. Her phone rings. It's Rita, telling her that King did well through the night with no further complications. The danger seems to be lessening. This is the best news ever.

Richard joins them at the breakfast table. He's wearing a suit with his American flag pin, his Texas state pin, and his Wright's the Right Choice campaign pin proudly displayed on his lapels. She notes his aftershave is strong.

"What's your schedule today?" She attempts small talk, her way of melting his anger since she refused to have sex with him. They should, at the least, be cordial with one another.

"Too many meetings to count. You could go with me." His eyes peer above the rim of his coffee mug. He offers a slight smile.

"Only if I can bring Matthew. Lola has classes this morning."

"Gabby, you know that's not possible. The campaign route is no place for a child. I would need extra security to keep him safe. Remember last Christmas when that crazy vet shot Amanda?"

Quickly, the scene shows up vividly in her mind as if in a movie— it was late afternoon, standing on the steps of city hall, the gun firing, the crowd screaming, and the blood blooming on Amanda's white fur coat. She shudders.

"You're right. I just want you to know that it's not because I choose not to come; it's that, as a mother, I have obligations. Someone needs to be a parent."

"Before we start the day dumping blame on one another, let's make a pact."

She raises her eyebrows in anticipation of what he will say next.

"We're both under a lot of stress. Me, in these final days. You, with your dad and whatever you do." He flips his hand in the air.

She allows his tone and gesture to slide so as not to interrupt his thought, biting the inside of her cheek.

"Let's forget about yesterday, the whole deal with Amanda. Wipe the slate clean. This is the countdown. The final days for achieving our goal." His eyes sparkle. "Please, can you do it for us, especially for King? He needs to believe that we're united, especially now." He reaches for her hand across the table. "What do you say? For us?"

She nods.

"Okay then." He retrieves his phone from his pocket and opens it to his calendar. "Ideally, you need Lola to keep Matthew every day and most nights. If Lola can't, you need to get someone else. It's really important as we near the finish line."

"Here, give me your phone, and I'll make a list. I'll check with Lola first. I can let you know later today which events I can definitely make."

"*Definitely* make? Let me be clear. I need you by my side at all events."

"Richard, it's not that simple."

He scratches his head. "Call an agency. Hire someone for a week twenty-four/seven.

Lola can train them. It's not that difficult, Gab. This should have been done weeks ago. You knew this week would be important—the most critically important."

She stands. "What about Daddy? I must take care of him."

"Rita can take care of King. Heck, there's Stan and Marie…Jamie and Rusty. From where I sit, your daddy is in excellent hands. I'm the one who's flying solo." He points to his chest.

Immediately, he waves his finger in the air. "On second thought, it would be good to have Matthew at the park tomorrow for the ribbon cutting. Everyone loves kids. What could be better than a kid at the park? He'll be an asset. I'll text Amanda and tell her to get an extra security guard, one just for Matthew."

"Now he's a commodity. Anything for a vote."

"Ladies and gents, young and old alike, mellow when there's a baby nearby. Accompanied by his own security guard, he'll be fine."

"Do you think it's wise to bring Matthew front and center? What if reporters snoop and find out he's your son? Maybe we should ask Daddy before we go with this idea. Matthew's eyes resemble the King side of the family, but his nose and mouth are yours. It's risky. With only a few days to go…"

Before she can finish her thought, a car horn beeps. Richard stands. "That's my car. Check with your dad about Matthew. Text me ASAP so I can get that security guard hired." He gives her a quick peck on the lips. She drops his phone into his outstretched hand.

"I'm off. You have my schedule. Surprise me. Come campaign with me this afternoon." He tilts his head and shows her that familiar puppy-dog face. "Do your daughterly duty and pay a visit to King this morning. Be with me this afternoon." She's certain this is his way of making up and closing the door on yesterday's incident with Amanda—as if it's forgotten history. He's already displaying his great charisma, which seems to work on most women because they frequently scream and plead for his attention at campaign rallies.

She nods. He waves, going out the door.

CHAPTER 27

G abby campaigned with Richard for the next three days, which
included taking Matthew to the ceremony at the park. Today,
she accompanies her daddy to the ranch after being discharged
from the hospital. She hadn't convinced Richard that it was best for
her to leave the city, but she made the case that family takes priority
even in politics. It would be good for the press.

The news media had gotten wind of King's hospitalization, and
when he was pushed out in the wheelchair, they were waiting on the
curb near the hospital's front door. They thrust their microphones
in his face, asking questions over each other, and some were filming.
She stood beside her daddy, smiling, being as polite as possible with
Matthew in her arms. As Rita pulled their SUV to the entrance, he
answered more of their questions than Gabby would have liked.

At last, she voiced "doctor's orders," helping him into the vehicle
for the drive to the ranch. She and Matthew followed behind in her
car. In her rearview mirror, a trail of reporters followed, so she phoned

Rusty to ask him to post wranglers at the gate to keep these intruders out.

Her daddy's discharge is her escape from the political scene. She's tired of the meetings, the people, the smiling, and the schedule. How Richard has done this for nearly two full years is beyond her thinking. However, that doesn't excuse his behavior. His little back-office escapades with Amanda are a deal breaker. Richard may still be her fiancé to the public, but she'll never share his bed.

Besides being five days before the election, this is the last weekend in October, so it's also Halloween. In the city, Halloween attracts strange folks, and weird stuff happens. During last year's celebration, several streets near the capital were blocked off due to a bomb scare. The scare became real when the K-9 unit found the bomb hidden under the suspect's costume. Incidents such as this reinforce her desire to protect Matthew by leaving the capital city for the security of the ranch. Her daddy's discharge has provided the needed excuse.

CHAPTER 28

The King Ranch, two days later

The lake view from her front porch always provides a respite. Even on her most harrowing days, sitting here communing with nature calms her soul. Last evening, she took her painting supplies and blocked in major elements on the canvas, determining the position of the horizon line, lake, and sky with her paints.

Earlier in her career, her abstract artwork followed the trendy style of New York City's modernism. Today, with her skills fine-tuned, she returns to the realism style of her youth. Closing her eyes, she brings her fingers to her necklace and moves her treasured trinity knot charm back and forth on its chain as she remembers her early days growing up on the ranch.

On the eve of each birthday, her mother encouraged her to paint a scene to portray the past year. Her bedroom walls became her diary, depicting the most significant events in her youth. She rendered cattle, horses, flowers, and rainbows. She painted her crown after she was voted Rodeo Princess, and she painted a heart with a rainbow to represent her first kiss. When Anna died after battling breast cancer, Gabby painted a lone trinity knot on that wall—like the one on her necklace—adding this last scene to her mural, a tribute to her mother.

The year following her mother's passing, Gabby painted different versions of this knot on canvas, creating an entire series as she worked through her grief until finally landing on a place of acceptance. One painting from this series became a favorite of both her and Brett, and it hangs above her fireplace. Every time she walks into her house, it's a reminder that brings her peace. The trinity knot remains a special symbol to the King family.

Finished with her stroll down memory lane, she redirects her attention to her easel and squeezes fresh paint onto her palette. The oily smell of the paint redefines her purpose as she breathes deeply. Quick to begin painting before the sun's first rays poke through the clouds, she prays to capture the colors in their finest splendor. She hopes for divine intervention to guide her brush almost effortlessly across the canvas as if God himself were the creator, and her brush, his vehicle. She looks to the horizon with her steady hand and says, "Universe, grant me wisdom."

She paints for guidance, clarity, and beauty, swirling her brush into the blue and applying it to her canvas. After the lavish blues, she follows with various shades of lavender and, finally, deep pinks, fading into a light peach. Deep in concentration in her effort to portray the morning sky at its best, she hums gospel songs, ones her grandmother taught her many years ago. She is void of anger, sadness, and anxiety; instead, she's content for the first time in weeks. No big revelations are present about her future or give insight into her relationships. Instead of the wisdom of enlightenment, the universe offers silent peace.

She stops painting, drops the brush on the palette, and steps away from her easel as the sun's rays beam above the horizon. Its bright light overtakes the sky's previous colors and now appears light blue. The scene she wishes to paint has vanished in mere seconds and now exists only in her memory.

In the past, painting has given her solutions to her problems. She continues to stare at the freshly painted canvas, rubbing her chin. Searching for answers, she pinches her lips together. She scans the colors and notes the varied shades as they overlap. The painting needs more work, but the sunrise is depicted beautifully. What has she missed? She throws her hands up, then rests them on her forehead—thinking, thinking. Perhaps no answer is the answer. Could it be that simple? She's where she's destined to be—at the ranch, her home, her resting place.

A jingling noise breaks her thoughts. Ryder runs up the steps to her porch and rubs against her legs.

"Hey, buddy, good morning." After petting him, she looks up, squinting as the sun shines in her face, following the lane toward Stan's house. If Ryder is here, Stan is close by. A whistle sounds from the opposite direction near the lake.

"No treats," Stan yells. "They'll spoil his breakfast." He stops and leans over her porch railing. "You're up early."

"I'm painting the sunrise."

"I gathered that. It sure was a beauty. I watched the sun chase the morning star away."

"The morning star?"

"You missed it? From the dock, it was right over there." He points to the northeast. "Yes, Venus is both the evening and the morning star."

"Why didn't I know that? By the way, how early were you out there?"

"I had trouble sleeping, so after tossing and turning and disturbing Marie, I needed a change." He looks away.

"Care to share?"

He lowers his eyes and shakes his head. "Can I take a look?" He joins Ryder on the porch and steps around to view the painting."

"Impressive."

"Thanks. So, tell me what you like about it." She studies his face.

"It's tranquil, relaxing, more like a sunset than an energetic sunrise."

She nods in agreement. "Nice. I thought the same. Painting was serene and relaxing."

Stan turns to leave. "Come on, Ryder. Time's a wasting."

She touches his shoulder. "Stay for coffee, please?"

"No can do. I'm working the ranch today. King must be feeling better. He's barking orders from his chair. Rita says to ignore him, but Rusty knows better. This time, your old man got lucky. I'm glad he pulled through."

"Me too." She pinches her lips together. "We really should talk."

Stan looks down at the sapphire ring on her finger. "As long as you're wearing his ring, we have nothing to talk about." He steps off the porch. "Marie's making breakfast. She's a good cook." He tips his Stetson and grins. "Come, Ryder, time to go."

As she watches him stride down the lane, his limp is barely noticeable. A sadness hovers over her like a dark cloud on this sunny day. She wrings her hands. Surely Stan knows her hands are tied until after the election. It's her job to keep up the charade. Watching him go puts a frown on her face. She's disappointed that he didn't stay.

CHAPTER 29

It's midafternoon before Gabby puts Matthew down for his nap at the main ranch house. Jamie and King offered to babysit so she could ride Lady. Earlier, she shared lunch with her daddy. She skipped talking about her relationship troubles and kept the conversation light. His face had more color, and his sense of humor was intact, but there was one thing different about him. He had engaged with Matthew more so than before his heart attack. Was that the result of his brush with death, or, in all fairness, because at nine months, Matthew can sit, and he loves being held with a book where pictures of animals keep his interest? Whatever the reason, it makes her happy they are building a relationship. She took photos of them together to include in Matthew's baby book for him to appreciate in the years ahead.

As she closes the bedroom door, the baby monitor in hand, her cell phone vibrates.

Amanda's picture flashes on the screen. She answers.

"Richard wants to know what color dress you're wearing to the dinner tonight. Amanda pauses, then says, "He needs to coordinate his tie."

Gabby says, "I got Daddy out of the hospital yesterday, and I'm spending today with him."

"The dinner's been on your calendar for a week. You're expected to attend." She pauses again. "I'll transfer you to Richard."

"Hey, Gab, I only have a minute. Tonight's dinner—black tie or the gray?"

"Richard, I'm with Daddy at the ranch. He's only been home twenty-four hours."

"Rita says you're going out riding. Final days, Gab. We discussed this. I need you."

She is going against Ella's advice. "I'm sorry, Richard. I'm staying here another night. I'll be back tomorrow." She bites her lip, thinking of the scowl he's making.

"Gabby, we've been through this a hundred times."

She remains quiet.

"Okay, very disappointing." The call is abruptly disconnected. She imagines she has given him an excuse to sleep with Amanda again tonight. Does she care?

Gabby hands King the baby monitor, leans over his lounge chair, and hugs him. "I love you, Daddy."

King looks up with his wise eyes. "Richard is not happy?"

"No, he's not. I'm staying here with you." She rubs his shoulders. "It's a dinner. He'll talk politics the entire night. He won't miss me."

"It's the aesthetics, princess. The cameras will miss you. He's right; you should be seen as a couple." He pats her arm. "But I'm glad you're staying. I'll speak with him."

"That's not necessary."

"I can smooth things over. I noticed a bit of tension between the two of you at the party. My guess is that he feels insecure because of Brandon. He is the spitting image of Brett and has a successful and interesting career."

She remains quiet.

"Gabby, should he be?" His tone is serious.

"Should he be what?" She leans closer, getting to his level.

"Worried that you're taking an interest in Brandon."

She stands and crosses her arms over her chest. "I can't believe we're having this conversation."

King rubs his chin. "You did take off Sunday morning to attend the car race."

"To be with Richard. Isn't that what all of you wanted?" She shakes her head. "Unbelievable."

"He spoke with me about it. He saw you dancing with Brandon at the dedication—thought you were dancing too close, especially when you rested your head on Brandon's shoulder. It's like you were acquainted. Maybe the newspaper got it right—that photo with you and Brandon holding hands across the table."

"Really, is that what Richard thinks?"

"It is. I must say it does paint a convincing story."

She feels the fire. Richard is preparing his case by creating a scenario where she's the one with fidelity issues. She has spared her daddy this conversation because of his health, but now it seems all gloves are off, and Richard has been on the offensive.

"If anyone should be worried about aesthetics, it should be Richard. It's ironic that he's concerned about me when he shows up with Amanda, who's drunk half of the time and has sex with him at the office. Just this Sunday, I caught them. There's no shame. I would be an utter fool to stay in a relationship with him. The psychologists call it *projection*."

He rubs his chin. "I know that Richard…let's say…has issues."

"I can't believe you're making excuses for him. The infidelity should have stopped when he put this ring on my finger."

King opens his mouth to speak.

"Don't give me that 'boys will be boys' crap. I'm your daughter. You should be worried about *me*. My feelings…" She closes her eyes. "I'm so sorry. Here you are, recovering from your heart attack. We shouldn't be talking about this now." She takes a deep breath and kisses the top of his head. "I'm sure that after the election, things will be different." She's glad he doesn't see her eye roll. She's heard similar comments from him before about tolerating Richard.

"That's my girl."

She fakes a smile. "Have Jamie call if Matthew wakes up."

Walking to the stable, she breathes deeply to release her body and mind from the anxiety the phone call and conversation with her daddy created. She won't ruminate on it and have it ruin her afternoon. She looks to the sky and allows the sun's rays to shine on her face, and her tension melts away. It is a glorious day.

Lady's ears perk up when Gabby enters the stable.

"Hey, girl, let's go for a ride. She leans into the mare's shoulder and places her head on her neck. Lady nuzzles her pocket. "Here you go. You haven't lost your sense of smell." She holds the apple for Lady to eat. "Ok, let's get your bridle and saddle."

Gabby wipes her brow and adjusts the straps on the saddle one more time. She's out of practice. Motherhood has slowed her down—that, combined with touring for the campaign. Her phone rings. It's Ella.

"Hey, Gab, did I get you at a good time?"

"Sure, anytime you call is a good time. How are you?"

"I'm doing fine. Gracie's taking a nap, so I can talk. First, how's your dad?"

"He came home yesterday. He's doing great. I just left him. I'm going riding while Matthew sleeps."

"That will be fun. It's cold here in D.C. Sometimes I wish I was back in Texas. The weather's so much warmer there. "That reminds me, the e-mail invitation. Are you going?"

"Once again, I have no idea what e-mail you're referring to." As she talks, Gab leads Lady out of the stable and ties her to the corral fence next to the mounting block. "Fill me in."

"I'll cut you some slack since it was sent only twenty minutes ago. It's from Marie to the wedding party, inviting the bridesmaids to go shopping for our dresses and her wedding gown. The shopping trip will be in Houston in ten days, so she's scheduling it after the election but before Thanksgiving. It's great that she's inviting me, but we were just there for the engagement party, so it will be hard to make another trip so soon."

"I'm sure she'll understand if you can't make it."

"Gabby, can I ask you a personal question?"

"Since when have you ever asked for permission? What's up?" There's a slight pause.

"How do you feel about the wedding…about Stan and Marie as a couple?"

What is Ella getting at? I hate lying, but I can't be honest with her.

Okay, just the facts. "I was a bit surprised by the fast engagement and setting the date in less than six months."

"Go on."

"What more do you want me to say?"

"You didn't answer the question. How do you feel about them as a couple?"

"They've been living together for a year."

"Gab, but how do you *feel* about them together?"

"I don't know…"

"Okay, I'll start. I'm not so sure about them. Everyone knows Stan has always had feelings for you. It's been going on for years. I saw the way you were together the other night. But then there is Brandon. You were dancing cheek to cheek. Are you holding out on me?"

"No. Geez, Ella. You have some imagination." She props her brown cowboy boot up on the fencing, admiring the intricate stitching. The boots, a present from her daddy nearly two years ago, and this is her first time wearing them.

"Really? This is me, your best friend, the person you can talk to."

"Hey, Ella, can we talk about this another time?"

"You just said anytime was a good time. That means you don't want to talk about it because there *is* something."

"No, it means my time's limited. I can only ride when Matthew is asleep, so I really need to go."

"Okay, go if you must, and get some exercise, but we're not finished."

"Ella, you're impossible."

"I know you, and something's not right. I'll look forward to our talk. Call me later." She pauses. "Promise?"

Gabby steps up on the block. "I'm getting on my horse and hanging up now. Bye."

Gabby shakes her head. Ella's inquisitiveness and her history of keeping secrets are not the best. She won't confide in Ella again until after the votes are counted.

Signs of fall can be seen in the yellow leaves on the trees, and a few display a blaze of fiery orange. The golden grasses wave tall and come up to Lady's knees. In the distance, she hears the bellows of the cattle. She stops short at the top of the hill overlooking the pasture. The wranglers are putting out salt blocks, and Stan is riding the fence line looking for downed wire and broken posts. She's heard rumors that some of the damage was from illegal immigrants crossing through the property.

This time of year, fence repair is needed more frequently, and several dozen cattle have wandered away. During the summer, there's plenty for them to eat, so when they're found a few days later, no real harm is done. In winter, a damaged fence line can be fatal to the cattle because less grass is available for the cows who need to be fed daily.

Stan gives her a whistle and motions for her to join.

As she and Lady meander into the pasture, Stan waves for her to follow as he inspects the fence. They ride along it for thirty minutes before he stops and dismounts at a small grove of trees.

He ties his horse, takes her reins, secures Lady, and then helps her down.

"Why are we stopping?"

"Taking a break. I want to show you something." He spreads a blanket he's been carrying on the ground under a tree. Then he pulls himself up to stand on the fork of the tree's trunk and reaches high above his head to part the leaves, revealing a lone apple. "I've been watching this Gala apple for a week. It's a perfect specimen for the tree's second crop."

She peers up at the fruit, then watches as he twists it off the twig on which it grows.

"Catch," he says, throwing her the reddish-yellow apple. "It's probably the last of the season."

She clasps the firm fruit and brings it to her nostrils, taking in the sweet scent.

Stan jumps down from the tree and resumes his seat on the blanket. He retrieves his pocketknife, opens the blade, and cuts into the delicate flesh. "Here," he says, patting the ground. "Take a seat. Let's find out if this tastes as sweet as it smells." He hands her a wedge. "We're lucky the critters didn't eat it."

She holds up the slice with a raised arm as if in a toast. "Here's to the last apple." She takes a bite, then turns to him, licking her lip. "What do you think?"

"It's awesome. Our future could be the same," he says with a twinkle in his eye.

She furrows her brow.

"I'm going to go out on a limb." He looks up into the tree to emphasize his pun before facing her. "Run away with me."

She shakes her head, dismissing his declaration. "You're engaged to Marie."

He places his index finger on her lips, signaling her to stop talking.

"I already explained that. Bear with me…just listen." His eyes are pleading, and her heart leaps when he takes her face in his hands.

DonnaLee Overly

"Together, we make a great couple. We work toward common goals. Look at what we have accomplished together."

She looks away because his intense gaze makes her uneasy. Her heart races.

He releases his grip. "It would be amazing." He takes another bite of the apple.

She takes off her cowboy hat and wipes her forehead. "Right now, Daddy's health is my primary focus, and then there's the election. I need to get through the next few days. I need to do it for him. He's worked so hard to get Richard into this race."

"I can tell you're stressed, but I needed to try again...to persuade you...I need you to see this through my eyes, but let's change the subject. Hey, I'm glad you came out today."

She runs her fingers through her hair. "Me too. I love being out here."

"Earlier, after dismounting, it looked as though you were limping."

"I shouldn't have worn my new boots. I have a cramp on the side of my foot. It was silly to put them on and ride without breaking them in." She pulls at the shiny brown boots.

"Here, let me see." He ignores her protests. "Trust me." He pulls off her boot. She lowers to lie on her back, and he pulls off the other boot. "You're in for a treat. I've read about this stress reliever. Tell me if it works." He positions her feet on his lap and massages both in tandem with his strong hands. "How's that?"

"Feels great."

"A reflexologist told me that massaging the feet helps his clients become more receptive, allowing their intuition to untangle life's knots."

219

His voice is calming, and his touch creates an energetic current that slowly awakens her body. As her defenses collapse, a vulnerability overtakes her. It's as if he's exposed her, and she's naked. It's crazy, exciting, and scary at the same time. She doesn't want this to stop. He's a hypnotist, and she's mesmerized under his spell.

She's unsure how much time has passed when he asks, "How is that? Better?" He moves and sits behind her head.

"Heavenly," she manages to find her voice, returning to reality from her nearly orgasmic state.

He rests her head on his lap. He's so close she can smell the fruity odor that remains on his breath. He runs his fingers through her hair, gently tugging at the scalp.

"That feels nice, too. Are you trying to seduce me?"

"I hope it's working. We're together every day in my fantasies." He moves to lie beside her and leans closer, propping his head on his elbow. She doesn't object. If she pulls away now, she'll always wonder what it would be like. *Don't you owe it to yourself? To Stan?*

She leans into his kiss, releasing all inhibitions. Their tongues dance, and he pulls her on top of him and presses her tight to his body. She was a schoolgirl the last time she felt this giddy. But this is no first kiss with a high school crush; this is the kiss of a passionate man going after what he wants. She pulls away, breathless.

He holds on to her arm. "Stay with me. Make my wish come true." He pulls her down, and they face each other side by side. He kisses her again with even more passion. "I want you."

Thoughts run through her mind: *Live for today. Life is short. What would sex be like with Stan? Richard has Amanda. Should I have someone else?*

After the dedication ceremony in her driveway, Stan's kiss caught her off guard, then after she watched him drive away, she contemplated running after him to make love to him. Will the same be the case today if she stops now? Will she wonder, *what if?*

He raises her arms above her head, clasps them with his hand, and peers into her eyes. It's as if time stands still. She furrows her brow.

He reads her expression. "Nothing's wrong—just the opposite. I want to always remember us this way."

He leans in for another kiss and pulls on her belt buckle.

"Stop, I can't."

"Yes, you can. We can. I know what we have is real."

She pushes him away.

"Really? You're stopping? Unbelievable." He lies on his back and looks up to the sky.

"I'm sorry, I can't. I need to end things with Richard. It's not fair…to either of us." She pulls up to a sitting position. "I have feelings for you. I do."

"Exactly what does that mean? As a stepbrother? As a lover? I've been waiting for years." He sits up and gazes at the horizon, shaking his head. "Have it your way."

"What's that supposed to mean?"

"You'll figure it out. I pray it won't be too late." He stands, dusting his Stetson on his jeans before placing it on his head.

"Oh my, what time is it?" She jumps up in a hurry to change the subject. She checks her watch. There are two texts and two missed calls—one from Rita and one from Richard. "I'm a mess."

Stan erupts in a cynical laugh. "That's an understatement."

She combs through her hair with her fingers, removing pieces of dried grass. "What am I going to tell them? What about Matthew?"

"Matthew will be fine. Tell them the truth."

"Get serious."

"I am serious."

"Your mother will go crazy. It will be my fault for leading you on."

She tucks her shirt into her jeans. "Rita has pulled me aside more than once to tell me to stay out of your life, to let you move on with Marie. She hates me."

"I love you, and that's all that should matter."

"I have to stay by Richard's side until the election. We talked about this."

"That doesn't mean I agree. I hate seeing you with him." He pulls a piece of grass out of her hair and places it between his teeth. "You're right about one thing; we need to get back. We have a thirty-minute ride ahead of us."

Quickly, she pulls on her boots. In contrast to the calm earlier, she's confused and unsettled.

He holds Lady's reins and helps her mount. "I've always known. Now, you know too. You had to feel it. You're searching for something that's right in front of you. Promise me that when you're standing next to Richard on election night with the confetti and balloons falling, you won't get sucked into the prestige, won't get lost in the limelight. Remember this. Pick us, Gabby."

Her phone interrupts. "I should go." She answers the call. "Hi, Daddy! It's been a gorgeous day. We lost track of time. I've been help-ing Stan check the perimeter." There is a beat of silence. "Yes, it's okay for Matthew to eat ice cream. Not too much."

She observes the man standing close. For a brief second, she searches his eyes, finding disappointment. "You're a good man, Stan." Her attempt to cheer him up fails.

He cups her face in his hand. "Remember today, a lost opportunity. I'll move forward with Marie. If you change your mind..." He turns away, mounts his horse, and heads back to the ranch.

CHAPTER 30

With a confident smile, Richard waves to the people standing in line at the conference center to cast their votes. They cheer and yell well-wishes. It's early morning, and it's raining. It will be a long day, and history proves there is less voter turnout in inclement weather.

Gabby holds a large umbrella to shelter them from the rain as Richard shakes hands and nods in agreement as though he has anticipated their remarks. She sticks close to his side and plays the role of the attentive fiancée. The cameras flash, and the reporters impatiently take turns interviewing the man predicted to be the next governor of Texas.

This election day will determine Richard's future. Years of preparation will culminate with this vote. The campaign team has diligently worked during these final two weeks. Amanda reports that tens of thousands of phone calls were placed, more than two thousand tweets written, hundreds of Facebook posts posted, and many You-

Tube videos uploaded. College kids worked the downtown campus and surrounding streets, handing out fliers and speaking with people to convince them that Richard is aware of their views and challenges and will work hard to represent them after he is elected. Today, many will hold signs near prime voting centers, although they will adhere to the electioneering law by keeping the mandated distance of one hundred feet away. It takes teamwork, and each has his unique duty.

After casting their votes, a mob gathers on the sidewalk at the exit, expressing an attitude opposite from the supportive crowd who greeted them upon entering. Gabby looks down, avoiding eye contact but can hear the political slurs and personal attacks at the mention of Harold Green, the opposing candidate.

Richard's large frame surrounds her, tucking her under his arm, and they closely follow the security guards who lead them to the limo waiting at the curb. Some of the protesters bang on the limo's hood and pound on the glass windows. The driver inches away slowly, allowing protesters to step out of their path.

After making his appearance at the polling place and casting his vote, the local police had advised Richard to hole up in a hotel and be as invisible as possible until after the polling places closed. Taking their advice seriously, the Kings rented the penthouse suite at the hotel, so they could all watch the election coverage together and in privacy.

Richard looks at her with a wide grin. "So many people. It's a good sign."

"It's intimidating—the yelling and the harsh words. Why are they so angry?"

"You're focusing on the bad. Focus on the cheers and chants. There are two sides to politics. You'll get used to it." He pats her hand.

She's not sure why anyone would willingly subject himself to this life.

"Hey, we had to vote and make it public. It encourages others to vote. Now, time to celebrate." He reaches for the champagne bottle and pops the cork. "We did everything we could. Now, it's time to sit back and watch the votes get counted."

"Richard, it's not even 9:00 a.m. I shouldn't. You shouldn't."

He hands her the champagne flute. "Today will be the first day of our new life. Here's to you, Gabby. I'm glad to have you by my side."

"Here's to you, the next governor of Texas." They clink glasses, and their eyes lock. Richard offers a quick kiss before snuggling lower in the limo's back seat.

CHAPTER 31

King and Rita are out and about this Tuesday morning even though they voted by absentee ballot a few weeks ago. Against doctor's orders, Rita drives King to the Capital Hotel. She knew better than to plead her case since it only made King more determined to have his way. Giving in reduces his stress level, thus better for his health. For several years, he's worked hard, devoting time and money, and has hopes for a favorable outcome with a win for Richard. No heart attack is going to stop him from participating in the festivities. She'd rather watch today's events unfold from the seclusion of the King Ranch, but it's not about her. If King were asked, this would be his dying wish. Here they are, right in the middle of the election madness.

◇◇◇◇◇◇

The Capital Hotel is located on the main street through the city, and the penthouse suite overlooks the state capital and the governor's mansion. Tonight, the after party, complete with an anticipated acceptance speech, will be in the hotel ballroom on the ground floor.

Extra security was put in place two days ago, which included scanning for bombs and checking the fingerprints and credentials of all hotel employees. Only guests with an active room key are allowed in the elevators, and the stairs are monitored by two guards each.

Gabby and Richard arrive and enter the suite with the security escort.

"Hey, Daddy, Rita…we're here. There's my boy."

Gabby holds out her arms to Matthew, who is gripping Lola's fingers to toddle about. Gabby rushes to pick him up. "Hey, precious." She swirls him around. "Thanks, Lola. It's a bit crazy outside."

"You're back earlier than I expected. I'm meeting my friends on campus. We're doing our best to bring in the votes. Then, I'm joining the rest of the team at headquarters." Lola grabs her jacket from the back of the chair. "I'll see you later, probably around 5:00 p.m. Is that good for you, or do you need me earlier?"

"You can make it later. We're staying right here…instructions from our local men in blue. It's like we're on house arrest. Have fun and be safe." She laughs as she closes the door behind Lola. Lola has been a godsend.

King and Richard are deep in conversation, positioned in front of the television, tuned into the local news station in hopes of getting hourly updates on voter attendance around town.

Rita walks over to Gabby. "I ordered coffee and Danish. It's going to be a long day. I thought we could go over the wedding details, so we're on the same page. This election stuff is getting old, don't you agree? Marie and I sat down a few days ago. It's going to be magnificent, such a beautiful time of the year for a wedding."

She sits down at the table with her notebook in front of her. "We're missing your RSVP and Ella's for the girls' trip to Houston. Everyone needs to be there. We're going to make a weekend out of it. I assume you're in." She checks her notes. "First, I reserved a private room at the Houston Club for lunch on Friday. Then, shopping at the bridal boutique on River Street, you know, the one where all the celebrities shop. Then we'll have a short break before having dinner and a night at the theater. It will be sort of a bachelorette party weekend." She takes a sip of coffee. "Then, Saturday, we're going to that huge bridal shop just outside of town—that one on TV. I called and e-mailed to get on the show. Lord knows we have the money to make it worth their while. And they certainly would want to make an episode with you in the wedding party, fiancée of the governor." Rita looks up for her approval.

"Wow, is this what Marie wants? She doesn't seem like the type for all of this. I figured her to be practical and down-to-earth." Gabby feeds a piece of Danish to Matthew as he sits on her lap.

Rita's eyes sparkle. "I gave her my ideas, and she didn't object. Basically, she said that all she cares about is getting married to Stan. Isn't that so romantic?" Rita's stare is piercing. "Will and Ella got married so fast that I was deprived of planning. I'm going to do it right this time because it will be my last chance."

"How many guests are you inviting?"

"That depends on today's outcome. If Richard wins, or should I say *when* Richard wins, he'll need to make and keep contacts. Wayne says that a spring wedding is a perfect place and time to keep the momentum going. It's the ideal situation—no room for controversy over politics. At least three hundred, five hundred, maybe more. It's too early to tell."

"I can't imagine that Stan is good with all of this."

"Oh, Gabby, all Stan needs to know, and all he cares about is that he's getting married. He'll leave the details up to us." She points her finger at Gabby. "Don't go filling that boy's mind with anything different. You can do whatever you like for your big day. This isn't your wedding. This is Stan and Marie's wedding. I'm counting on your support." She puts her pen down on the table and leans forward. "This is delicate, but I feel inclined to say it. I know that you and Stan, let's say, share something special. You're moving on with your life, and Stan needs to do the same." She raises her eyebrows, then pats Gabby's hand. "I know I can count on you." She nods, stands, and turns away quickly.

Gabby's stomach falls, telling her that something is wrong. She closes her eyes, remembering her day with Stan out riding—the apple, the foot massage, their passion…she stopped before the lovemaking. Every day she imagines a different ending. Her *what-if* scenario plays out over and over in her mind. How can Stan share anything close to that with Marie?

Coming out of her daydream, she lifts her eyes to Richard—his impeccable dress, precise haircut, and well-rehearsed mannerisms. Visually, he's perfect, so what is wrong with their relationship? She lowers her eyes to Matthew. His profile is his father's, from his cheek down to his chin. The knots in her stomach tighten. She has been waiting for the election, this very day, but has she waited too long to claim Stan? Should she stay with Richard and allow Stan and Marie to marry?

As the day continues, the group in the penthouse suite grows in numbers. Jamie and Rusty arrived midmorning, and Stan and Marie came after the morning session at the equine center. Steven Prime pops in for a chat. He's always a pleasure and livens up the room with his full-bellied laugh. Gabby is happy her daddy has a friend. He brings them lunch—pizzas and deli sandwiches—and distracts them from the election by giving a full update on the Mercedes team at the F1 race held this past weekend in Mexico. With his arrival, some of the tension that had slowly been building has lifted.

Richard spends most of the afternoon on his cell phone, pacing back and forth across the suite. She assumes he's on the phone with Amanda, stationed at headquarters. Stan is glued to Marie's side, listening to Rita endlessly review plans for the spring wedding. His interest bothers Gabby. She never finds him glancing in her direction, which makes her heart sink. But she had her chance.

As the afternoon progresses, Gabby notes her daddy has grown quieter and appears tired, so when she excuses herself to put Matthew down for his nap, she invites him to join. Propped up with pillows in the bed, her daddy flips through the picture book with Matthew on his lap until both nod off in slumber. Carefully, she carries Matthew to his carrier, then covers her daddy with the throw from the chair.

She exits, closing the door quietly behind her, and accidentally leans into Stan.

"Gosh, you scared me," she whispers.

He wraps his arms around her waist and kisses her on the back of her neck. "I know I shouldn't."

She wiggles out of his grasp. "Stan, stop it. Don't you have more wedding plans to discuss?" She pushes his arms away.

"Oh, do I note a touch of jealousy? You have the power to stop it. We can walk out arm and arm and declare our love to the world."

"Today? Are you crazy? Don't you think there's enough tension?"

A noise sounds behind them, like someone clearing her throat, and they turn.

Rita has her hands on her hips. "What's all the whispering about?"

Think fast, Gabby. "We don't want to wake Daddy and Matthew. They were so cute together. Daddy was reading to Matthew, and they were asleep in no time."

"Then you best talk elsewhere, don't you think? Perhaps, join the others." Her voice is harsh, and she pulls Stan's arm, dragging him away.

Gabby bites her nails and wonders how much of their conversation Rita overheard.

CHAPTER 32

Later that evening in the hotel suite, Gabby looks at the sophisticated woman in the mirror, dressed in a royal blue dress with a matching jacket. Her four-inch heels give her height to stand level with Richard's chin—perfect for photographs with Richard presented as the powerful authority figure and Gabby, his wealthy, supportive partner. It seems that society has more confidence in taller people. She's convinced the presenter of this theory must be a man who never spent the evening in spiked heels.

To complete her outfit, she's been instructed to wear a strand of pearls. Not the iconic choker Barbara Bush fashioned, but a strand of pearls hanging inches below the neck to trigger memories of the successful Bush legacy. Texans loved the Bush family, and now it's important for Texans to love Richard Wright.

Upon entering the living room, her daddy looks up, then nods in approval. When Richard crosses the room, he approaches with a sparkle in his eyes and bestows a kiss. She greets him with a smile as he takes her hand. Amanda stands at a distance, wearing a long face, and turns from the happy couple to stare out the window as she brings her wine glass to her lips. Witnessing her reaction, even though the two women are at odds, Gabby feels empathy for the campaign manager who professed her love for her client.

She observes the rest of the assembled family. Rita and Marie sit on the couch, and Lola entertains Matthew nearby, building towers with wooden blocks.

She searches the room further. "Where's Stan?"

Rita is quick to answer and places her hand on Marie's knee. "He went back to the ranch with Jamie and Rusty. You know Stan is not much for city life. There's always work to be done on the ranch. He gives his best to you and Richard on your success." Rita smiles.

Gabby reads a lack of emotion on Marie's face. Why would Stan leave without saying good-bye?

The doorbell rings, saving Gabby from a reply. Two men are at the door.

"Surprise!"

"Brandon?" she says in a breathless voice.

"I told you I would be back after the race in Mexico. From your expression, you didn't take me seriously. May we come in?"

"Yes, of course." She initially thought the figure in the hallway behind Brandon was another security guard, but she was wrong. "Sorry, Mr. Prime, please come in. It's so nice to see you again."

"Steve, please. No formality here. It's a night not to be missed. My, my, you are a sight. I would say, dressed for success, are we?" He gives a belly laugh. "Congratulations." He hugs her tightly before holding her at arm's length. "We're in the big time now." His eyes gleam.

Gabby walks them into the room. "Daddy, Steve is here, and he brought Brandon with him."

King stretches his neck to look around the corner. "Hello, come in. What a surprise!" He jumps up from his chair for a handshake. "Thanks for coming. Get your drinks and have a seat." He nods toward the bar. "It looks like Richard here will be giving his acceptance speech soon." He pats Richard on the back. "We may be a bit premature, but it looks promising. We need to wait until a few more districts count their votes." King points to Amanda, who is settled at the desk with the computer. "I hope Green doesn't draw this thing out. He needs to concede so our boy can give his speech before half of Texans slumber in their beds."

With everyone glued to the television, Gabby takes Matthew from Lola to feed him dinner. Between spoons of chicken and rice and away from the others so her conversation is private, she punches Stan's number into her cell. It rings and rings. She thinks the click she hears is directing her call to voicemail—instead, Stan answers. "Hey."

"Hey, yourself. You left?"

"I did."

"Miss you."

"That's good to hear."

"Why did you leave?"

"Rusty needs help at the ranch."

"Is that all?" He remains quiet. "Did I do something wrong?"

"Gabby, what do you want me to say…congratulations to you and Richard? I can't stay to watch you slip away."

"I explained this to you."

"Let me paint the picture…you'll be up on stage with Richard, holding hands and smiling, and all of Texas will think that you are the perfect couple."

"Stop, I get it. I really do, and I'm sorry."

"I don't want your apology. I want you…"

"Stan…"

"Hey, I'm gonna go."

"Stan—"

The line disconnects. She closes her eyes, knowing the truth behind Stan's words. Texans will think that she and Richard are the perfect couple. That's exactly the campaign image her daddy wants to instill in voters. The same plan she agreed to a few months ago by welcoming an escape from the painful memories of Brett's death in exchange for the political life standing beside Richard. Traveling down this path these last two months has been harsh.

Taking Matthew out of his highchair, Gabby holds him on her hip, joining the others in the main room. Brandon rushes to her side. "There you are. Are you ready for a win?" His voice is cheery.

"It doesn't matter," she says softly so the others don't overhear.

His eyes are wide. "What are you talking about? Of course, it matters. This is your future."

She smiles with tight lips. "My future. What if this future is not what I want?" She looks from side to side to ensure no one is eavesdropping. "This is Richard's life, not mine."

"But you're here." He cocks his head to the side. "I'm confused."

"I've been convincing myself this is where I'm supposed to be. However, lately, I feel sacrificing my life for the greater good bears too high a price. I can still do good things with great purpose without the Wright name leading the way."

"Such as?"

"I can fulfill my purpose in helping others at the equine center. And I can do more—I can promote literacy and help feed the poor."

"Yes, you can do all those things. Heck, Gabby, you can do whatever you set out to do. Tonight, Richard will reach a goal he set years ago. Tonight, your fiancé will be the next governor of Texas." The excitement in his voice contrasts with her facial expression. He shifts his weight. "For what it's worth, you don't look or sound like a woman who's happy her fiancé is about to take the biggest step in his career."

Can she confide in this man she barely knows? He seems sincere, and she is desperate for a friend. If he's serious about being family, maybe it's time to pull him into her inner circle. She leads him out of the room into the hallway. It's a good thirty minutes before they return to join the others.

Richard turns up the television. "It's happening. Yeesss!"

His excitement prompts King to look up. "The margin shows Richard in the lead. It has expanded to 20 percent." King clears his throat. "El Paso is the only big city left to have their votes counted. We have friends in El Paso, so I'm not worried. Our team at the university reports the majority will vote for Richard. They love his platform on education reform. They can relate to him because he's close to their age, and with Gabby on his arm, they see a young, classy, successful couple."

Richard turns and walks toward Gabby, then puts his arm around her and draws her in close. "He's right, you know. We are the dream couple. Are you ready?"

She nods in agreement but bites the inside of her cheek.

Brandon takes a seat next to Marie. "Hi, remember me?"

"Of course, Mr. Race Car Engineer. We had such a good time at the bar. Closed the place down. We should do that again sometime."

"I'm good with that. Name the place and time; I'll be there." He clinks his glass with hers.

"I'm glad you're here. It gives me someone to hang out with."

"I'm glad I'm here too. Stan left you alone on a night like tonight...his loss is my gain." He clinks his glass against hers again and winks. "Let the party begin."

CHAPTER 33

Hours later, room service is ordered. The food falls second to the numbers that flash on the television screen. Matthew was put to bed, and Gabby nurses her second glass of white wine. She wasn't going to start drinking before the results; however, holding a glass keeps her from biting her nails.

The waiting grows more intense with each passing minute. Both her daddy's and Richard's phones have been ringing literally nonstop. Amanda's fingers have yet to cease dancing on her computer's keyboard. Every now and then, after an outburst by King in either favor or disapproval, Rita chimes in, voicing her concern for his health.

Gabby pays close attention to the dynamics of interactions in the room. She eyes Brandon in deep conversation with Marie and Richard with Amanda as they huddle close to King.

Suddenly Richard leaves the room with his phone to his ear. A short time later, with great enthusiasm, King yells, "Turn up the volume. Quiet, everyone!"

On the television, Harold Green stands at a podium, waiting for the crowd's cheers to dissipate. Gabby notes a permeating stillness as all eyes focus on the screen.

In a strong voice, Harold Green says:

My fellow Texans, we have come to the end of a long journey. The citizens of Texas

have spoken. A few minutes ago, I had the honor of calling Senator Richard Wright to

congratulate him on being elected the next governor of the state we both love.

This campaign has been long and difficult. His success commands my respect for

his ability and perseverance. However, through it all, he managed to inspire the hopes of

our youths, who had wrongly believed they had little at stake or influence in the election of a governor. This is something I deeply admire and commend him for achieving. Thank you all, and God Bless Texas.

With the first taste of announced victory, excitement fills the air with cheers and clapping. Richard embraces Gabby, lifting her off her feet and swinging her in the air, lighting her face with a genuine smile. Next, they gather for congratulatory handshakes accompanied by pats on the back. Everyone's hard work contributed to this victory. Glancing around the room of smiling faces, Gabby notes a seemingly serious Amanda. When Amanda briefly glances in her direction, Gabby walks over.

"How can I be of help?" She nods at the perky blond in her four-inch spikes.

Seconds later, as if on radar, Richard steps forward, occupying the space between the two women. "Gabby, Amanda, everything okay?"

"I came over to congratulate Amanda and thank her for running a successful campaign."

Instead of acknowledging the compliment, Amanda brings a screen up on her phone. "Richard, I need a moment. We should review tonight's schedule."

"Good idea." Gabby holds on to Richard's arm as if claiming him. "I'll hear the schedule firsthand. No need for Richard to repeat. He must save his voice."

He rubs his forehead, then gives Amanda an approving nod. "Right, you're right. Amanda, what's our schedule?" He winks, then places his arm around her waist.

Maybe he was being honest when he said his behavior could be blamed on the frenzied, busy campaign schedule. Will tonight's win change their relationship? Will Amanda dig her claws into Richard more now that he has power and prestige? Is this the life she wants?

CHAPTER 34

Gabby stands close to Richard in front of the roaring crowd. Banners displaying her freedom painting wave in the air, horns blow, and balloons that had previously fallen from nets above are being batted, soaring them through the air once more. All rejoice in the party's victory with the campaign song blaring. The atmosphere permeates a gaiety that's infectious. Nothing could have prepared her except for Stan's earlier forewarning. She understands his absence.

The lights of the TV filming equipment shine in preparation for Richard's acceptance speech. The audience lights blink and then darken, followed by a hush that rolls from the front of the convention center to the far corners.

As he stands behind the podium, Richard's voice sounds clear and strong.

"We're victorious."

He grabs Gabby's hand and lifts their arms in the victory sign, and the crowd erupts in unison. He waits and waves, making eye contact with key supporters and occasionally giving a nod or a thumb's up. The accomplishment, sweet for Richard and her daddy, brings unexpected satisfaction. Each piece of falling confetti, a symbol to represent a task such as a phone call, a meeting, or the words and efforts of thousands that have made this evening a success, and she gives appreciation by closing her eyes and saying a prayer. Scanning the crowd, she chokes back tears as she finds her daddy's cheerful face. He is living his dream.

No one could have possibly prepared Gabby for the celebrations on victory night—the waves of excitement, the fanfare, and the deafening noise of horns. Hours later, she wonders when the ringing in her ears will cease. Back in the hotel suite, she collapses on the couch and removes her heels. Inspecting her feet, she finds blisters. It's 5:00 a.m. She hasn't pulled an all-nighter since Matthew's illness eight months before.

Richard leaned heavily on Gabby in the elevator returning to their room. Yes, the celebration patrons expected him to share a drink. Hopefully, the press will extend some grace in today's news since it's not every day that a man gains the title of the governor-elect of the state of Texas. Throughout the wee hours of the night, he handled himself with dignity, and she was proud to be on his arm. She peeps into the bedroom, and his snores confirm his rest.

CHAPTER 35

For Gabby, the days following Tuesday's election whirl away as though carried by a cyclone. Contemplating a drive to the ranch is out of the mix since Richard's presence receives higher demand than ever. Honoring her daddy's request, she attends every event. Gabby scratches her head. She was mistaken to think that the election would be the end of this craziness.

Her original plan was simple—regardless of the outcome, she would break up with Richard after the votes were counted. Political life is not her future, and she's angry over his affair with Amanda. But here it is, one full week later, and his engagement ring rests on her finger. The reflection of light on the facets mimics her thoughts as she twists the ring. She notes how some catch the light and sparkle more than others. It's an analogy that can be applied to life. Some events shine while life's secrets hide in the shadows. Both are necessary to make life complete.

Like the changing light on the ring's facets, the dynamics of her relationship with Richard have shifted. Since campaign headquarters closed and Amanda packed her bags en route to her next job opportunity, he has done a one-eighty turnaround. As though trying to make amends, he has been attentive and considerate, such as giving Gabby affectionate hugs, holding her hand in public, and bestowing quick kisses throughout the day. Unbeknownst to him, she checks his phone periodically, and it appears that Amanda has gone silent. It's puzzling since she anticipated a fight from the blonde for Richard's affection. This battle would have ended quickly as she was prepared to walk away.

However, with each of Richard's simple acts of kindness, her heart melts a bit, and the one thing he did to get more than a flicker of forgiveness was to take an interest in his son.

A few days ago, Richard handed her a bag.

"What's this?"

His eyes sparkled. "Open it."

"It's not my birthday."

"Does it have to be your birthday? Sorry to disappoint, but it's not for you. It's for our son."

She was at a loss for words. He had never bought Matthew anything and was generally forbidden to refer to him as his son. Since Matthew's birth, he has never offered any financial assistance or inquired about Matthew's progress in growth or ability. In other circles, he would be considered a deadbeat dad, but to everyone's knowledge, except a small handful of family members, including relatives, they have kept the secret that Richard is Matthew's father. Richard has played his role to perfection.

Inside the bag was an animal picture book.

Then Richard picked Matthew up from his carrier, held him on his lap, and carefully turned the pages while making animal sounds. As he

held Matthew on his lap reading, her heart softened with ripples of for-
giveness. Finally, she got a glimpse of them as a family, not a perfect family,
but few, if any, families fit that mold. Family has always been her dream,
and doesn't Matthew deserve a relationship with his father?

She swore never to have sex with Richard again, but when he cud-
dled close that night, visions of their family danced in her mind, and
she gave in. Her simple plan had hit another detour.

From Richard's recent behavior, she's convinced King must have
intervened on her behalf. Her daddy is quite persuasive and has been
known to twist arms. Did he lecture or possibly threaten? Did he pay
Amanda to disappear? If Richard's new attitude is not genuine, it will
not last, and he'll revert to his old ways. That will cause her emotional
damage.

With her relationship renewed, she carries guilt, so she avoids
Stan. Their time under the apple tree brought enticing feelings she
had long thought she was incapable of experiencing. Stan made her
feel alive, a woman both desiring and desirable. It was romantic. She
doesn't have this sexual excitement with Richard and doubts that,
with their history, they will ever recapture that aspect of their relationship again.

Stan's words surface: *"I've waited and watched the drama of your*
life unfold. Choose me. If not, I'll go forward with Marie." According to
others, Stan has held a torch for her since they first met at his mother's
wedding to King. She'll lose him forever if she chooses the role of the
governor's wife.

Wife. The word makes her stomach roll. At Stan's and Marie's
engagement party, Richard spoke of the grand wedding they would
have, one that all of Texas, if not the world, would marvel at. She's
newly committed to forgiving him for Matthew's sake, but she's hard-

pressed to include Richard in the same sentence as "family." The gap between them has narrowed, but it's still evident. *Damn, having sex with him clearly sent the wrong signal. What was I thinking?*

Her worst-case scenarios are coming to life. *Be careful what you wish for.* The old saying tumbles over in her head. She had wished for Richard, her, and Matthew to be family. Now Richard is trying, and she's confused because of her awakened feelings for Stan.

Her second cause for concern, as if this isn't enough, is that she's spending less time with Matthew. Lola is writing her final class reports, limiting her time to babysit. Even though Gabby first cringed at Richard's suggestion to hire a nanny, that's exactly what she has been forced to do. Sharon, Rita's friend who recently lost her husband, voiced the need to fill her empty nights. When the offer came in, Gabby could hold out no longer. At least Matthew's caregiver is a family friend instead of a total stranger. During the interview, the woman was pleasant enough, and Gabby noted an experienced maturity as if nothing could rattle her.

Fulfilling her role as the governor-elect fiancé at public functions has made Gabby suffer separation from her son, and she secretly fears her little angel will forget her. However, this weekend's schedule, which is causing her to be an absent mother, is void of the political scene. It is Marie's bachelorette weekend in Houston and probably the main reason for Rita's motivation to help find a sitter. She has stressed the importance of this affair for the past month, which Gabby would skip if given a choice.

CHAPTER 36

Houston, Blushing Brides Boutique

Rita beams with the excitement of the moment. The highly anticipated Houston bachelorette party and shopping for the wedding gown and the bridesmaid's dresses is here. For Gabby, it's the start of the dreaded weekend. Gabby wishes Ella could have been there so she would have a confidant. However, with this event scheduled so close to the engagement party, it was impossible for Ella to attend.

A wedding should be a once-in-a-lifetime event. To Gabby's knowledge, this wedding lacks the most important, basic ingredient: genuine love. It's like baking a cake without eggs and flour. Who does that? Selecting a wedding dress weighs in as one of the most extraordinary moments in a young woman's life. One that brings tears to her eyes, a feeling so special it creates a lifetime memory. Does Marie love Stan, and is she aware of Stan's love for Gabby?

From Stan's confession to Gabby, she knows he's settling; however, Marie's feelings remain a mystery. Other than greed from the million-dollar prenuptial agreement, why would Marie consent to this marriage? Is she clueless? Does Stan touch Marie with the same intensity? She shudders, thinking about it.

A spark of jealousy fuels an existing flickering flame as Gabby imagines the what ifs smothered with droplets of regret. If she allowed her and Stan's lust to play out instead of listening to her inner voice of reason, Stan could be hers, and it would stop this charade. However, the bride is playing her role perfectly so far, providing evidence that perhaps the young girl is in love. It could be that she feels indebted to Stan for saving her life. Her ability to escape the human traffickers was truly remarkable on its own, but for Stan and Ryder to find her on the ranch's outskirts near death was a miracle. Gabby can understand how a young and vulnerable girl could confuse gratefulness for love.

Champagne begins to pour as Marie spends moments with her personal assistant, discussing the details of her dream dress, such as basic design, color, lace, and bling. In the meantime, Rita scans through the rack of dresses, choosing three that she describes as perfect for Marie's body type.

Rita made a rating system based on points on fit, color, design, and overall score. As Marie models, the rest of them are to give each dress a number, an idea Rita got from a television show.

Rita claps her hands to alert the small group. "Pay attention. Marie's coming out of the dressing room in a few minutes. Dress number 1. Get your papers ready. This is the Yves Saint Laurent." She clasps her hands together. "I can barely wait to see her. Marie will be the perfect bride—so young and pretty. Stan has made a wise choice."

Remarks like this one make Gabby's skin crawl. She gulps champagne, but no amount of alcohol will settle her uneasiness. She drains the final sip from the flute and refills the glass to the rim, careful not to let the bubbly overflow at the beginning of a long afternoon.

Gabby looks around the bridal showroom. She is one of four attendees. In addition to herself and Rita, there's Marie's mother, Rosa, and Marie's friend from school, Alexa. Both women flew in from San Diego last evening. All four sit on velvety cream-colored couches, surrounding a raised circular platform framed with six large mirrors covering the walls.

Finally, Marie makes her first entrance, and there are a few audible *ahhhs*. She waltzes in as if she's Cinderella entering the ball, exaggerating her movements as she sways from side-to- side before stepping onto the raised platform. She wears an off-white satin gown with beading on the bodice. She looks innocent, like a young girl playing dress-up as she lacks the cleavage to fill out the plunging neckline.

Gabby, reluctant to seem critical by showing a low score on her card, decides to give an inflated rating of seven. She glances at her companions and sighs in relief as Rosa gives the dress a six.

During the critique of this first gown, Gabby's phone vibrates, and with Brandon Matthews's name scrolling across the screen, she excuses herself and hurries to the opposite side of the bridal salon.

"Brandon, it's good to hear your voice."

"Mission completed." He sounds as if he's boasting. "I can't talk because I need to be with the team. We adjusted some valves on the engine. The time difference makes it tricky for a proper call, and I didn't want to leave a message."

"Mission completed? Does that mean what I think it means?" Her mind tries to process this shocking development.

"You were right. We'll talk more later. Glad I could help. Thought you would want to know."

"That seems fast."

"Lady asks, mission done. Simple. Bye."

When she returns to the group, drops of perspiration on her arms give her goose bumps in the air conditioning.

Rita furrows her brow and rolls her eyes. "It's about time. I can't imagine what could be more important than the task at hand. You missed our discussion on the YSL."

Gabby thinks fast. "I'm sorry. It was Daddy." She forces a smile, giving credibility to her lie, knowing that Rita will dismiss her absence if King's name is mentioned. With her disappearance excused, she exhales in gratitude and reaches for her champagne with a trembling hand.

"Carolina Herrera is the designer of the next gown. She designed Caroline Kennedy's, Bella Swan's, and Jessica Simpson's gowns," Rita announces, throwing her shoulders back as all heads nod approvingly. "I found this one on the sale rack. Heavens, it was twenty-five thousand—at eighteen, it's a real bargain."

Rosa raises her eyebrows as though in shock at the mention of the price. Marie's middle-class family can't possibly afford such extravagance. None of their conversations last night addressed the responsibilities of each family.

As Marie exits the dressing room modeling the second gown, Gabby's eyes tear. The cut of the dress conforms to Marie's body like a second skin. The gown is white with little cap sleeves and an elegant Chantilly lace bodice that flows the length of the dress to the floor. The classy, romantic style exudes Herrera, as if she designed the gown exclusively with Marie in mind. The dress rates a top score—easily a ten, higher if the scale would allow. The bride-to-be must feel the elegance and perfection the gown offers because she is glowing.

It's the most exquisite wedding gown Gabby has ever seen. She bites her lip, attempting to hide her emotions. The romantic vision of two lovers promising to have and to hold from this day forward and forsaking all others is the stuff of dreams. However, this perception is quickly replaced with one of ugly distortion and deception. A thought that steals her breath and darkens her soul.

The information Brandon shared in his phone call kidnaps the fairy tale's happily-ever-after-ending. She wipes the wetness with her napkin, hoping the others have been focused on the bride, oblivious to her outpouring of emotion. If they do notice, perhaps they will believe her tears are those of joy. They would be seriously mistaken. Rita could surmise Gabby's reaction to be driven by jealousy, which would be a closer bet but still not the real explanation.

Gabby's primary reason for her emotional outburst is concern over Stan's welfare. Following through with this wedding isn't in his best interest. It's ludicrous by any standard for these two to unite in matrimony. She must warn him.

Stifling her tears, she turns her attention to Marie, recalling Rita's words when they first entered the salon: "So young and pretty." Rita would take that back if she knew the true essence of the soul hiding inside the beautifully wrapped package. This is the opposite of what any mother would wish for her son.

In the hours that follow, Marie models dresses from other designers, but none can hold a candle to the Herrera. After negotiation, the store agrees to hold the dress without a fee for forty-eight hours. After leaving, the group's excited conversations center around this *perfect* dress.

Chapter 37

Matthews Horse Equine Center, a few days later

Gabby has given Sharon, the new nanny, time off since she worked the weekend. As soon as Gabby waved Richard out the door this morning, she packed her things, scooped up Matthew, and watched the city skyline disappear in her rearview mirror as she drove east to the ranch. Living at the hotel has stopped being glamorous. The increased security measures may sit well with the next governor; however, it doesn't work for a country-loving gal.

Richard will be unhappy with her decision, so she has decided to avoid an early morning argument. Since he didn't ask what her plans were for the day, she didn't lie. He will think her decision selfish, although she did check his schedule, noting that he'll be attending congressional committee meetings for the remainder of the week. An hour into her drive, she left him a voice message.

The mid-November day is warm and sunny, but temperatures tend to drop quickly after sunset. Gabby turns off the car engine and steps out, wrapping her shawl tighter to ward off the cold. To her surprise, the gardenias have been recently planted in a semicircular bed at the equine center's front entrance. At the far corner of the building, Stan leans on a shovel, laughing, and Marie kneels in the dirt, her smiling face turned toward Stan. If photographed, they could appear the perfect couple in a real estate magazine as if they were planting flowers in front of their newly purchased house. She undoes the buckles from Matthew's car seat and carries him on her hip.

"Hey, there," Stans says, the first to speak. "Do you like?"

"Like? I love it. How long have you been working out here?"

Marie smiles, her face glowing. "My 3:00 p.m. canceled, and

these gardenias have been wilted for days. They needed to be planted. We had fun digging in the dirt, didn't we, honey?"

Stan nods. Gabby sits Matthew on the porch and places some toys from his diaper bag within reach.

"I didn't want to make the beds too big. Are they okay? I can make them larger later if you'd like." Stan grins.

"They're fine. Perfect. Thank you for doing this." Gabby holds her hands as if in prayer to acknowledge her gratefulness.

Turning away from Marie, Gabby observes Matthew pulling himself to a standing position using the wooden railing surrounding the porch. Her little man will be walking soon. Here, unlike in the city, there is plenty of wide-open space for him to explore. Plus, it's good for him to play in the fresh air.

As the happy pair finish with the last plant, Gabby paces, rehearsing the difficult conversation she anticipates having with Stan. The sooner she gets it off her chest, the better. This urgency replaces her previous guilt.

She sits on the rocking chair near where her son plays and leans over to pick up a small plastic figure—a farmer wearing overalls and a green hat. She moves his arms away from his side and sits him on the tractor. She imagines his smile wider. The tractor makes a *vroom* as she pushes it toward her son. Matthew squeals with delight. She marvels at the innocence and joy of childhood wonders. Watching her son playing on the porch confirms coming to the country was the right thing to do. They're home and with family. She's looking forward to the precious days she'll have sharing Matthew with her daddy. His recent heart attack has revealed there are no guarantees of tomorrow.

Marie is first to speak as she and Stan approach the porch arm-in-arm. "Beautiful day."

Gabby stands. "It sure is. I'm glad to be here. The city life isn't for me."

"You'll have to get used to it. Richard will be spending more time there now than ever."

Gabby pinches her mouth with a tight smile.

"Hey, I got your text message. What's on your mind?" Stan knocks his Stetson hat back, allowing his friendly brown eyes to be seen.

Marie's presence changes everything. Her conversation is for Stan's ears alone. *Quick, Gabby, make up something fast.* "We need to discuss this center's end-of-the-year report."

Stan rubs his chin. "Can't that wait until tomorrow?"

She lowers her eyes and looks away.

"I know that look. Something's wrong."

Damn, he's perceptive—always has been when it comes to me.

"Something is terribly wrong." She nods toward Marie, who is playing with Matthew.

In a low, quiet voice, she says, "I can't discuss it now."

"Marie, do you mind staying here with Matthew for a few minutes so we can review items on the horse center's budget?"

"Sure, no problem." Marie smiles. "Don't be too long. We need a shower before dinner." She winks.

Stan grins and nods, then follows Gabby around to the stable.

As they walk side-by-side, he says, "Okay, spill it."

"I rehearsed this speech the whole drive here, and I still don't know where to start."

"Starting at the beginning is always good." His stare penetrates to her core.

"It's not that simple. Maybe today's not the right time." She looks down, making circles in the gravel with her shoe.

"Gab, really? Now I'm worried." He stops walking and holds her shoulders, looking into her eyes.

"I can't explain with you staring at me like that."

"The longer you delay, the more persistent I'll be. I know you. Just spit it out. I promise you'll feel better afterward."

She throws her shoulders back and takes a deep breath. "You can't marry Marie."

He raises his eyebrows. "You've got my attention."

She looks past his shoulder. "She's having an affair."

Nervous with the silence that follows, she furrows her brow. "Did you hear me? She's having an affair...with Br-br-br...Brandon Matthews."

He's as rigid as a statue—not a blink or a twitch. "And..."

"And...you can't marry her. She'll hurt you. You deserve better."

"Now, there's one thing we can agree upon. *You* would be my choice."

She's been holding her breath. Relieved that he's finally engaging, she can breathe again. "You can't possibly go through with the wedding. Don't you have any self-respect? She's fooling around with Brandon. If she's unfaithful now, it's a good indicator that your marriage is doomed."

He scratches his chin and grins before breaking into robust laughter.

"You're laughing?" She puts her hands on her hips. "What's so funny?"

"At the moment...you!" He laughs again.

She closes her eyes and thinks he is insane. "This is serious. I'm trying to help you."

He holds on to his stomach. "You...helping me? This is good, really, good. I haven't laughed this hard in a long time."

She's been troubled by Marie's affair since Brandon's phone call at the bridal salon. Thinking of her angst and the long hours that her heart has ached for Stan, her emotions unleash. Tears form and threaten to spill down her face. Overtaken by her anger, she turns away, shaking her head, thinking him foolish. He's heading for disaster. *You can't marry her. I'm trying to save you.*

From his reaction, her humiliation is monstrous. Previously, all she wanted to do was help him avoid a painful future. Now she wants to crawl into a hole and die. Unable to contain her frustration, the tears overflow. She runs faster.

"Gabby, stop. I'm sorry. Please stop." She can hear his limp as he tries to catch up. "Gabby, I'm sorry."

"Go away. Leave me alone." She turns and screams, "You're mean and cruel!" His reaction is surprising and confusing.

"Please, I'll explain." His heart melts seeing her tear-streaked face. "I shouldn't have laughed. I'm sorry." He fights his desire to comfort her in his arms.

Instead, he pulls his handkerchief from his pocket. "Here." He extends it as if it's a peace offering.

"Please, I'll explain. You caught me off guard. I shouldn't have laughed, and I'm sorry."

She sniffles and dabs her eyes.

"I'm touched that you care with so much passion. It's refreshing... actually."

His expression of deep concern sends a wave of sincerity.

"Gabby, I have prayed endlessly for your eyes to open. Today, you want to protect me? Spare me from heartache? You want to save me when you refuse to save yourself?"

She raises her head and stares with eyes as big as saucers. His expression changes in a split second. His brown orbs take on a dark hue as though possessed by a demon.

His voice turns harsh. "Maybe now, you can imagine the magnitude of my suffering watching you with Richard." He firmly grabs her arm as his pain surfaces, sending terror through her body. Through clenched teeth, he says, "It kills me…kills me to see you with him." He releases his grip. "You're nothing but a hypocrite." Her eyes confirm the hurt as soon as the words escape his mouth. His words are a dagger piercing her heart.

All color drains from her face. He closes his eyes as if to take his actions back. But there is no magic wand to reverse the hands of time. Her urgency to save him and not see her own situation released years of pining, causing his never-ending patience to erupt into a spew of hurt. The release is instantaneous and lacks inhibition. *What has he done?*

She steps back, giving distance. "Get away from me." She rubs her arms where he held her.

"I'm sorry, so sorry."

She brushes his hands away. "Don't touch me."

"Gabby, I'm sorry. There's no excuse, but let me…"

She rubs her arm. "Just go. I can't be near you. Go."

He abruptly turns and walks back to the horse center's entrance. "Marie, time to go," he yells, opening the driver's door to his truck.

Marie bends to give her good-byes to Matthew.

"Marie!" he yells again as he revs the truck's engine.

Before closing the passenger door, Marie extends a look to Gabby as if to ask, *what happened?* The tires spin on the gravel as the truck speeds away.

Gabby stands, baffled by his alarming rage, and watches the truck until it turns from the driveway to the main road. In all the years she has known Stan, he's been calm, never shaken. She has never doubted his intentions and has always trusted him. However, today his actions were appalling. His remorse is visibly sincere, but that doesn't excuse his behavior.

Today, it's like he's a maniac. She had predicted his anger when he found out about Marie's affair. However, she never contemplated that his anger would be directed toward her. A red outline from his firm grip marks her arm, but the pain is mild compared to her inner turmoil.

She picks up Matthew and hugs him, holding him close to her heart. She craves the comfort of unconditional love. Stan's words tumble around in her head. *Hypocrite.* What is she missing? *Save myself, save myself…from what?…the political life…from Richard…from Daddy?* It's a lot to process.

CHAPTER 38

King Ranch, later that same day

Gabby rocks on her porch with a sleeping child in her arms, watching the sun set. Finally, going over her circumstances for what seems like a thousand times, it becomes clear like a veil of fog lifting. Stan is right; their situations are the same. If Marie's unfaithfulness is inexcusable, why does Richard receive a free pass? What about his lack of commitment? With renewed objectivity, she can answer the question, *where is her self-respect?* She would argue that her affection for Richard stems purely from a sense of duty. Devoting her life to playing the role of the governor's wife to please her daddy is a big assignment. Chances are her odds of happiness and love would be greater if she joined a nunnery.

This one decision will carry consequences for a lifetime. In the list of her priorities, family has always held the top position. Her connection to this ranch holds a close second. It's true that with her false sense of duty, she got caught up in the excitement of the election's victory. She twirls Richard's engagement ring around on her finger, the symbol of a promise, a promise to love and respect. Stan's right; she's a hypocrite and a fool. She called out Marie's affair when in her heart, she cheats. She doesn't love Richard. Who is worse?

She tells Stan to have self-respect. Does she have any? The price of her commitment to Richard is one that she can't afford because it doesn't reflect her values. She kisses her son's head, wishing to be wrapped in his blanket of innocence. Suddenly it's clear. She knows what she must do.

She hears the crunch of gravel before she sees the dark silhouette approaching on foot. Seconds later, Ryder romps up the porch steps. She wraps Matthew's blanket tighter around them, bracing for the upcoming conversation.

"Gabby, I feel awful. Please hear me out. I wish I could take it back." He hangs his head.

She points toward the rocking chair, offering him a seat to join her. He gives a pinched smile as though in gratitude. "Please, forgive me. I'm so sorry."

She continues to rock and looks straight ahead. "You're right, you know. You've gone about it the wrong way, but you're right. I see it now. Truly, I do. I should thank you."

Even in the dusk of early evening, he sees the darkened bruise forming on her wrist. "I snapped. I've been frustrated for so long, and I know it's not...I would never hurt you." He sighs.

"You need to know Marie is nothing like Richard. She had too much to drink, and let's say that Brandon was encouraged. I'm sorry."

She bites her upper lip. "The one thing I am 100 percent sure about is that I need to be a mother to this little one. I'm going to spend more time here at the ranch with Daddy, Jamie, and Rusty. This place, along with my family, is my anchor.

Someday, I'll inherit the ranch, and there's no time like the present to learn the business. With that said, Stan, please consider this ranch your home as well—not just your house down the lane, but the whole ranch: the cattle, the oil fields, all of it. It will take both of us to work it properly. There are no better mentors than Daddy and Rusty."

She takes off her engagement ring and places it on the table. "I'll call Richard later tonight. He left me several angry messages because I deserted 'the cause' by coming here. It's over between us."

Stan sits forward in his chair. "I'm pleased that your plans for the ranch include me. I do love it, and it is my greatest wish to spend my days right here. However, I'm curious. Does breaking your engagement and your new enlightenment about your life's direction include a relationship with me?" His eyes speak in earnestness and sadness simultaneously.

"Could be. I'm not ruling that out." She reaches for his hand. "But if you must marry Marie this spring, that's on you. I'm not ready to commit to anyone. It's obvious that I'm a mess. I'm still grieving Brett's death. I've had a lifetime of people telling me how to live. Now, it's my turn." She smiles at him. "True confessions: I do have feelings for you, and our time together under the apple tree confirmed as much. However, a relationship wouldn't be fair to either of us right now." She raises her eyebrows. "I do wonder, though, what the outcome would have been if we had followed through on what we started."

Her smile elicits one on his face. "Really? Tell me more about that."

"My fantasy…I'll blush. Shame on you." She giggles.

His face lights up. "They say timing is everything. Full disclosure, Gabby, not only do I love you, but I love Matthew and the ranch. Remember that."

"If you follow through with your wedding, I may have to stand and object during the ceremony."

He smiles. "Mother would be really peeved."

She laughs, and he joins in.

He stands, then leans down, bestowing a light brush on Matthew's forehead. "I feel better."

"Me too."

"Come along, Ryder." He caresses her shoulder with a gentle touch. Her eyes follow him as he walks down the lane with a bit more spring in his step.

CHAPTER 39

King Ranch Graveyard, three months later

Spring arrives early, giving birth to new life after the stagnant winter months; trees bud, meadows burst with bluebonnets, monarch butterflies visit on their trek to the north, and newborn calves stand beside their mothers. Gabby dismounts before tying Lady to the wrought-iron fence that encloses the family graveyard. On her ride, she picked a handful of the abundant blue flowers and now places them by Brett's headstone. She squints in the bright afternoon sun, gazing to find heaven.

"Hey, Brett. I miss you. Sorry I haven't stopped by recently. I've been busy. I know that's a lame excuse, but it's true." She wrings her hands. "I brought some flowers. You loved the bluebonnets." She pauses. "It's taken a while to figure things out after you left, but I'm finally getting there. The big news is that I broke up with Richard. I know getting back with him was a terrible idea. You never trusted him, and you were right. It was a hard lesson. Daddy took it better than I thought he would. The world did not end."

She puts her hands in her pockets. "Stan and Marie were supposed to get married next month, but they broke up. Marie admitted that her infidelity voided their contract, and Stan's million-dollar check was ripped into pieces. I thought the contract was a silly idea. Since then, Marie quit her job at the equine center and headed to California to live close to her family. Rita's been pouting ever since their split, and she blames me for the reason she can't have her fancy wedding.

Daddy got tired of her complaining, so he arranged a dinner party and put her in charge. There's nothing she likes better than organizing a party." She gives a nervous laugh. "The President of the United States accepted the invite, so it will be a grand affair at the governor's mansion. I'll attend to drum up support for my literacy program. I guess it would be proper to say *our* literacy program since it's under the umbrella of The Brett Matthews Foundation.

Let's see, what else? Daddy lost twenty pounds. He looks better than I've seen him in years, and he's been the best grandpa to Matthew. Matthew loves the ranch, especially the horses. He reminds me of you, and I can hardly wait until he's old enough to ride. You would be a better teacher, but I guess that wasn't meant to be." Her voice trails off a bit, and she bites her lip.

"Daddy's heart attack gave me a new perspective on the future. Stan and I are going to run the ranch. With Stan's previous business and law degree, he's concentrating on the oil business by attending meetings with Daddy on drilling and sales. I'll be learning that industry one small piece at a time. Meanwhile, I'm following Rusty to learn the cattle end of the business. Earning the wranglers' respect has been challenging. I'm sure they're testing me. I'd appreciate it if you could whisper any helpful tips in my ear or, better yet, come down and kick their butts to get them in line.

Matthew's new nanny, Sharon, lives in our guest room. Since I'm working more, I need extra help. She's only been here a few weeks. Bo and the other new ranch hand, Rick, have eyes on her and vie for her attention. It's fun to watch."

She kicks the grass and sighs. "There's something else...I've been getting closer to Stan. He can't replace you, but he's a good man, and he's great with Matthew. At times, I'm jealous. My little man seems to prefer Stan because whenever Stan is in view, Matthew breaks into a wobbly run to greet him. It's really cute. I'm grateful he's a role model because Richard remains the absent father. Not a surprise. Maybe it's for the best in the long run."

She gets down on her knees. "Stan is kind and understanding. He's been very patient. I don't know how I would have survived these past two years without him. I think we can be happy...together." She looks down. "Well...just thought you should know."

She outlines Brett's name on the stone with her forefinger. "I'm sorry you never got to meet your twin. Brandon is nice, and he's family. He has promised to be there whenever I need him. He reminds me so much of you. He's been spending more time with Matthew, me, and the ranch. We're the only family he has." She giggles. "I'm teaching him to ride. He's slowly getting the hang of it. You would have liked him." She stands and brushes the dirt off her pants. "I'll always love you. I need to go on with my life, for Matthew's sake... and for my own." She looks to the sky, blows a kiss, turns, and then walks away.

CHAPTER 40

King Ranch, a month later

I t's dusk, with just barely enough natural light remaining for Stan to set up his telescope for the solar spectacular, the title he has coined for the occasion. Gabby unfolds the blanket, plops the cooler onto one corner to weigh it down, and places the docking station on the other. Soon she rocks to the soft sounds of The Moody Blues. "My dad grew up with this stuff. It's pretty good."

"It's the perfect night for viewing. Unseasonably warm, no moon, no wind. Close to perfect. Look, the evening star has graced us with its presence."

He backs away from the telescope's eyepiece and gives her a wink. "In a short while, the sky will light up with hundreds of stars visible to the naked eye and thousands more with the scope."

He sits on the blanket next to her. "You had a good day?" His smile radiates, putting a glow on his entire face.

"Yes, did you see the headline?"

"I thought you stopped reading that stuff."

"I couldn't help myself. Today's paper's headline: **Governor Wright Voted Most Eligible Bachelor in Texas.** It seems that breaking our engagement has created a buzz of publicity. The article said that Richard has been photographed with a different woman on his arm every day for the past three months. Each woman interviewed expressed interest in becoming Texas's next first lady. More power to them since I never wanted the job. If I had listened to my heart, it would have saved me months of confusion."

"No regrets?"

"None. This is the happiest I have been in two years."

He opens the champagne, and the cork pops loudly, causing Gabby to jump.

"Sorry, what's the occasion for the champagne…a celebration?"

He hands her a glass and clinks it with his own. "Do you know how many times I've tried to get you out here? The heavens are spectacular, you know. You're spectacular. Let's toast to you."

"To me?"

"Yep, to you. You just said you're the happiest you've been in a while. That's worth toasting. You're doing great with the business… the ranch and the horse center. And you're an awesome mom. Miss Gabby, I applaud you for taking control of your life."

"You're making me blush."

She gazes up. "Look at the sky. The stars came out all at once. Now, there are too many to count." She shivers. "The temperature drops fast this time of year."

He snuggles up closer, placing the blanket around their shoulders. "Better?"

"Much."

He lifts her chin, and his eyes search deep as if reaching her soul. Her heartbeat quickens. A powerful universal force speaks directly to her, and suddenly, it's as if the stars align for them. His lips find hers, and she eagerly accepts. Tonight, she's ready to explore a new adventure with Stan.

Then, in the sky above, a star shoots across the sky, leaving a long trail.

Stan points. "Quick, make a wish."

"Wishing on a shooting star is considered good luck—like a promise that your wish is guaranteed to come true." Her voice is excited.

He smiles and holds her tight. "My wish has already been granted."

And they lived happily ever after...

The End

CPSIA information can be obtained
at www.ICGtesting.com
Printed in the USA
BVHW042117250723
667820BV00001B/25